Good Hurt

BOOK 1

SUMMER ROBERT

Also by Summer Robert

The complete *Good Hurt* Series:

Good Hurt (Book I)

Good Hurt: Splinter (Book II)

Good Hurt: Salvation (Book III)

CONTENT NOTE: *Good Hurt* contains some themes that may be distressing to readers, including references to an attempted sexual assault of the female main character that happened during high school (discussed briefly as part of her past), depression and thoughts of hopelessness, momentary desire to cease living, narcissism and narcissistic traits, and a direct family member battling cancer and undergoing chemotherapy.

This book also contains detailed and explicit two-person sex scenes that include elements of degradation and masochism kink.

To the fuck me all better girlies, get on your knees and beg.

CHAPTER 1
Addison

A BLAST of frost-laden air against my face causes my breath to hitch and I struggle to breathe as the icy mist billows around me. Why won't my feet move? Why am I still standing here, subjecting myself to the permafrost of frozen vegetables, staring at the endless bags of frozen peas as my eyes glaze over? The chill nestles over my exposed shoulders, causing my teeth to chatter, but the bags of frozen peas have ensnared me and I can't pull away.

"You should ice it," he said yesterday as he planted the bag of frozen peas against my bruised arm. My knees nearly buckled. The memory of his fingers grazing against my skin ignites a wave of something hot and coiling in my stomach – the kind of something that has me convinced I might either throw up or hyperventilate or both. The absolute myriad of fantasies I have conjured up in my head about this boy could write a novel, several probably, which is why I'm finding it hard to do the sensible thing and shut the door.

"Excuse me," a male voice cuts in beside me and I jump, tripping over my feet as I almost topple over. "Can I get in here?" he asks, tilting his head toward the frozen vegetable case blocked by my body. My startled reaction must have seemed disproportionately overpronounced because the man looks at me as if I've lost my mind. *I suppose I have.*

"Oh, sorry," I say, embarrassed. "Of course. Hot day outside." I offer him a small grin. True, it is a hot day but the heat index is not to blame for my present frozen pea fixation.

No, it was *him*.

Twenty-seven hours and thirty-three minutes ago I was sitting at the kitchen counter in my house, scrolling through social media and doing my damnedest to go unseen. I was disgusting. Sweaty, smelly, hadn't shaved my legs or armpits in over a week, no makeup on, hair pulled back in a bun, wearing yoga shorts and a sports bra, displaying all my physical insecurities and zits and sparring bruises for the world to see. I always look like that after Krav Maga and if I'm being honest, I love it. I wear those bruises with pride. My mom hates them of course, wincing each time she spots a new mark on my upper arm or outer thigh. Once I came home with a sizeable bruise on my jaw – the sight of the purple and brown splotches blooming across my face drawing tears to her eyes. I thought she might make me quit, but she knows how much the practice means to me.

Krav Maga saved me that day three years ago. The day when everything changed. When *I* changed. So, she lets me continue even if it means I come home looking like I've been in a street fight.

Normally, I don't care how I look but with my brother Ethan home, having just graduated from Harvard, I should have expected *him* to show up sooner or later with the constant revolving door of Ethan's friends now littering our house. In high school, he played lacrosse with Ethan *and then* also went to Harvard with Ethan *and* joined the same frat as Ethan, so I should have known he would be around sooner or later this summer.

Asher.

Asher Aves.

He was two years Ethan's junior and luckily (or unluckily) for me, Asher has also been my obsession since I first set eyes on him at a lacrosse game.

My eyes flutter just now thinking about our initial encounter. Encounter is rather a strong word. Spotted from afar is a better description.

I had gone to one of Ethan's Saturday morning games at the behest of my mother. I fucking hated going to those lacrosse games and I would sit scowling beside my bubbly and chatty mother as she gabbed with the other adults, dreading the end of the game when all the parents would linger on the field, making small talk with one another, while they waited for the boys to emerge from their post-game huddle.

I would stand there at her side and wait with no one to talk to save for my precious text messages. I felt self-conscious and reluctant as the players began to mingle into the throng of parents, glorious in their lacrosse uniforms, joking with one another as their sweat-slicked hair clung to their temples. Their collective scent was overpowering, like salt mixed with grass and traces of boyish smelling body spray. They oozed confidence and charm as I stood there, bashfully looking like a fucking leper, praying no one would notice me. And for the most part, no one did.

I was shy. I always had been. Ethan was the gregarious one. I had been content with my voyeurism, blending into the shadows like a nobody, until the day I heard Asher Aves say my fucking name.

"Mom, this is the new kid I was telling you about," I remember Ethan saying, chipper as ever. "He transferred schools a few weeks ago to ours, but he's originally from Chicago."

"And does the new kid have a name?" my mother teased.

"Asher," the new kid responded, in a voice so deep and masculine it made my ears tingle. "Asher Aves." He extended his hand to shake my mother's, and I felt a strange twinge of curiosity burst behind my now too-wide eyes. *Who was this?*

"Such a pleasure to meet you Asher," she cooed. "Oh, and this is Ethan's little sister, Addison. She's in eighth grade. What grade are you, Asher?"

A flush of the most searing, scarlet heat splashed across my face as if someone had hurled a bucket of boiling liquid on my head. I could feel how hot I was, my skin sizzling. Never had I been so mortified.

"Sophomore," he said.

"Oh, so you'll be a junior when Addison's a freshman. How lovely."

I shot her a look like *what in the fuck are you doing, woman?*

"Is that so?" His voice was smooth like melted chocolate as his gaze swept in my direction and landed on *me.* For a fleeting moment, the world stopped. His eyes were a shade of olive-green-hazel I couldn't place, his dark brown hair verged on the precipice of black, and he looked like the kind of forbidden prince you read about in fantasy books.

"Mom, we have to go. You cooking tonight?" Ethan cut in.

"Barbequing. And you're welcome to bring your friends."

"I'll be home then," Ethan smiled, giving her a kiss on the cheek as he always did. "Asher, let's go."

He gave my mom a polite smile. I had almost escaped with my dignity, until he glanced my direction one last time. "Nice to meet you, Addison," he said as a wry smirk spread across his lips.

A croaking noise rose from my throat. I don't know if he heard it. I pray he didn't. I don't know what I was trying to say. *Bye? Nice to meet you too? See you around?* What came out was a jumble of all those attempted words and then some, causing my mom to glare over at me with a look that was a mix of *what the hell kind of choking baby cow sound was that* and *do I need to call an ambulance because you're five seconds away from flatlining?*

The entire encounter haunts me to this day.

Often, I would see him at my house with Ethan but was too awkward and timid to do anything but hide in my room. Ethan was always bringing friends over, having pool parties. Even after he graduated high school, our house would fill to the brim with cocky, adolescent high school boys whenever Ethan was home… until it didn't.

Until my incident.

After it happened, Ethan stopped bringing his friends around.

And, well…

Shit, I wince, realizing I've been standing in the frozen foods aisle for lord knows how long. *Why am I here again? Right, cancer popsicles.*

CHAPTER 2

Addison

"MY SAVIOR," my mom says to me as she peels off the thin plastic wrap from the fruity ice pop. They remind me of the popsicles I would eat when I was a child – the sugary, skinny ones that only come in cherry, orange and grape flavors. *One of the few foods I can tolerate,* she always tells me.

"How was treatment today?" I ask.

"Not the best, not the worst," she answers, the bite of her popsicle slushing between her teeth.

"Did you see the doctor?"

"I did."

"And?"

Her momentary aversion of my gaze tells me all I need to know.

"He wants me to see this specialist in New York City. I'm on the waiting list for an appointment. They told me there are always cancellations the week of July Fourth so I went ahead and optimistically booked a plane ticket."

"That's perfect actually," I say. "The train from DC is only about four hours, so I can meet you in New York."

"Are you sure you want to do this thing at Johns Hopkins?" she asks.

Here we go again.

"Mom, we have already been through this."

"I know, I know. It's just… it's your last summer before Harvard. Wouldn't you rather stick around LA and relax?"

"Mom, you know how competitive the biochem major is at Harvard. Remember what the admissions person said? The big pharmaceutical companies only hire the ones who were at the top of their class. Plus, you know I want to be invited to the research fellowship at Harvard next summer, and they only offer spots to the top five percent of freshmen enrolled in biology. Getting into that summer program practically ensures you'll get one of the big pharma research jobs. I need to do everything I possibly can to give myself a leg up. So no, relaxing this summer is not an option."

She looks at me sheepishly, and I suddenly feel bad for subjecting her to yet another one of my condescending diatribes about this research fellowship spot next summer. But she knows how important this is to me. How am I supposed to find a cure for her if I don't have the resources and backing a research job at one of the big pharma companies would provide?

"I was afraid that would be your answer," she laments. "You know your father and I can't fly to Johns Hopkins with you, right? We have a wedding in Santa Barbara that weekend. Your father's nephew, remember?"

"Yes, I remember and I'm eighteen, Mom! I'm an adult. I'll be fine. Besides, I've flown many times before by myself."

I see the skepticism in her eyes. "When is the last time you had a… you know?"

She doesn't want to say it, so I'll say it for her. "A panic attack? It's been at least six months, maybe longer." *A lie. My last panic attack was two weeks ago.*

A warm smile spreads across her face. Not a smile of pity or concern, but of pride. And then… sadness. "My little girl is all grown up and now she's leaving me."

"Mom, please." I wrap my arms around her, careful not to hug too tightly – her treatments cause her to bruise so easily.

She pulls back, wiping away bits of moisture now pooled in the corners of her eyes. "Your brother is out by the pool with his friends. You should join them."

I huff a laugh. My mom and I share an enjoyment of annoying Ethan whenever possible. "You know how he gets with me around his friends. You just want me to fuck with him!"

"Language!" she says, walking toward the living room. "And yes," she smiles, giving me a devilish grin over her shoulder.

———

I love nothing more than fucking with Ethan. He hates, *loathes*, when I parade around in front of his friends. I understand his concern, I really do. But what happened to me was three years ago. Sure, I may not be anywhere close to mentally or emotionally healed. But I made a promise to myself last year to put myself out there. And I don't intend to break it.

Oh, this red bikini will do just fine.

The concrete scorches the soles of my feet as I saunter toward a chaise lounge by the pool. Only four of them today – Wyatt, Leo and Asher, the latter spiking the ball over the net toward an awaiting Ethan as I walk past. The blazing midday sun, clinging to every inch of my skin, feels like my own personal spotlight as I drape my towel over the chair without even realizing the ruckus from the pool has abruptly stopped.

"Addison, what the fuck are you wearing?"

Ethan. Right on cue.

"Fuck off, Ethan," I shout back.

"Aren't you supposed to be packing for nerd camp?"

"Aren't you supposed to have a job?" I snap.

He tosses the ball up into the air, catching it on the way down. "I do have a job, it just hasn't started yet," he smirks.

I roll my eyes, not that he will notice from behind my sunglasses. Of course, the prodigal son has managed to find a job that doesn't start until after Labor Day, giving him one last summer of freedom. I hate how he barely has to try. Life seems to come so easy for him. Of course, he would get accepted to Harvard even though he barely lifted a finger in high school, save for lacrosse. Of course, he would join a fraternity and party nonstop in college but still manage to graduate at the top of his class and score some big-time job at a venture capital firm in San Francisco. *Of. Fucking. Course.*

"Ouch!" A wet ball smacks against the exposed skin of my stomach. *Fuck, that hurt.*

"I'm serious, Addison, go fucking change."

Oh, so it's going to be one of these days again, when well-intentioned, protective behavior starts to feel a lot like blame. When Ethan's text messages to *"be more careful"* if I'm wearing something even the slightest bit provocative in a social media post start to feel scolding. If he only knew the battles I rage in my own head to reclaim a smidgen of the confidence I lost after the incident three years ago. How I clawed my way out of a pit of self-loathing, inch by painful inch, the small scar under my jaw a constant, mocking reminder, just so I could make my *"don't worry, I'm fine"* mask more believable. I do not need his bullshit subconscious blame for what happened to me *because it wasn't my fault.*

"Ethan, leave your sister alone, for fuck's sake. Let her live her life."

Thank you, Leo. I can always count on him for comedic relief and to call Ethan out on his shit. It's too bad Leo didn't get into Harvard. Ethan could have really used a friend to check him on his god complex these past four years.

I try not to notice Asher hoisting himself out of the pool, water rolling off his perfectly chiseled, tan abdomen, and I definitely try not to notice the glaringly obvious bulge protruding through his sopping wet swim trunks. I see him towel off in my periphery but don't anticipate the sudden thud of his towel landing on the lounge chair next to mine.

"You going inside?" Ethan hollers.

"What do you want, Ethan?" Asher asks. I sense annoyance in his tone.

"You know what I want," Ethan shouts.

"Leo?" Asher asks.

"Yes please," Leo answers.

"I'm taking the day off," Wyatt adds.

"I know," Asher retorts. "You've only already told us five hundred times today."

"Such an asshole," I hear Wyatt mutter.

"Can I bring you a drink, Addison?"

Wait, is he talking to me? And does he mean like a drink, drink? I've had alcohol before but never in front of Ethan and certainly never in front of Ethan when he's with his friends.

"She's underage!" I hear Ethan yell.

"Jesus Christ Ethan, are you her fucking keeper or something?" Wyatt scoffs.

"He's always this bad," Leo confirms.

"I'm fine, thanks," I manage to say, irritated I have to wait for the entire peanut gallery to say their piece before I can even get a word in. Ethan, Wyatt, and Leo start up another game of bash the ball around the pool while making as much noise as possible and I settle back into my tranquil session of vitamin D infusion. At least Ethan's not bothering me about my swimsuit anymore. I peek down at my abdomen to see a crescent-shaped pink welt starting to take form from the wet ball he threw at me. *Fucking asshole.*

"Still bruised I see."

"Jesus! Don't scare me like that!" I jolt, sitting up to snatch the ice cold can pressed against my upper arm.

"She can't have that!" Ethan shouts.

"It's a soda, Ethan, chill the fuck out," Asher shouts.

I hear the pop of cans opening as I take an unbothered sip from mine.

"You didn't ice it like I told you to yesterday," he says in reference to the bruise still on my bicep. His tone is quieter as he lowers down into the chair next to me, like he doesn't want the others to hear our conversation. I'm forced to give him a side-eyed glance because my entire body tenses at the sound of his deep voice. For the life of me, I can't move – my arms and legs have gone leaden.

"Hmmph." I give him a closed-mouth chuckle. I can feel all the moisture in my mouth vanish, my throat begging me to take another sip of soda, but I can feel my hand beginning to quiver. In no world can I raise the can to my lips without spilling it all over myself.

"What's nerd camp?"

Can someone please explain to me why this boy is all of a sudden talking to me? Shit, now I'm going to have to respond with actual words.

I swallow. "It's not nerd camp," I croak, clearing my throat. My voice is embarrassingly hoarse. "It's a summer program at Johns Hopkins that pairs undergraduate students with PhD candidates to help them with their thesis research. It's mostly for undergrad students who are pre-med or pursuing a degree in biochemistry like me. You don't have to be a student there to participate."

"And you can still do this program even though you haven't started college yet?"

"As long as you are enrolled for the upcoming academic year, yes."

"It sounds…"

"Don't say nerdy," I cut him off.

"Ambitious?"

I desperately wish for an ounce of Ethan's charisma in this moment. Instead I just shrug.

"I guess," is all I can think to say.

"Is this from the ball Ethan threw at you?" He grazes the now obvious welt on my stomach with a slow, soft stroke of his fingertip, and the sensation of his touch rolls over me like a crackling hot fire. Goosebumps from the feeling of his skin against mine flare across my body.

"Asher, you know Ethan doesn't allow us to talk to Addison," Leo yells from across the pool. I should be more annoyed by Leo's interruption. But it gives me a chance to compose myself.

"I'll allow it," Ethan responds. *Now* this *annoys me.*

"Why?" Leo wails with genuine confusion.

"You know why, Leo," Ethan answers.

"Because he's not a dick," Wyatt interjects.

"Asher?! Are we talking about the same person here? Because Asher is the biggest dick out of all of us!" Leo protests.

"I think you mean *has* the biggest dick," Asher says as he leans back, kicking his feet up. The contrast between this version of his voice – loud and unabashedly cocky – and his soothing, gentle voice from a minute ago catches me by surprise. I feel my face flush to what I can only imagine is a concerning shade of crimson. And why am I blushing so uncontrollably at the mere mention of his penis size? I can practically feel the confidence seeping off him as he leans back against the arm he's bent behind his head.

Do NOT look at his swim trunks, I scold myself.

"Seriously though, Ethan. Would you rather your sister be with Angry Asher over there or me, a sweet, cuddly teddy bear?" Leo continues.

"Who calls me angry?" Asher sneers.

That booming, harsh voice appears again, and I'm starting to understand Leo's point of view.

"Literally everyone!" Leo hollers. "You are the definition of asshole! Matter of fact, if you search for the definition of 'asshole' online, you'll find the name Asher Aves in the search results."

"Well, on second thought, Leo kind of has a point," Wyatt interjects. "You do have a bit of a… reputation."

"Is that so?" Asher responds, his nonchalant tone sending another wave of tingles across my goosebump-covered body.

"Do you disagree?" Wyatt asks. "I mean, come on, Asher. There is a reason why every pledge in our frat is terrified of getting on your bad side."

"I'd say I'm more 'brooding' than 'asshole' but I understand nuances aren't your strong suit, Leo."

"What the fuck is that supposed to mean?" Leo scoffs, sensing the joke at his expense.

I smirk. Having known Leo since I was a kid, I know exactly what Asher means and I don't even have to look at Asher to see the satisfied grin plastered across his face.

"Okay, *prick*," Leo seethes. "Let's ask Addison. Addison, would you rather get with a *brooding* asshole or a cuddly teddy bear?"

Wow, this took an unexpected turn.

"For fuck's sake," Wyatt groans. "She doesn't want to get an STD, Leo."

"I don't have STDs! But also, condoms, dummy!"

"Oh my god, ENOUGH!" Ethan shouts, water violently splashing everywhere as it collides with his fist. "Stop talking about fucking my sister, who is literally sitting ten feet away. Addison, will you go change already? Clearly these animals can't control themselves around you in a fucking bathing suit."

There it was. The blame.

I try not to let my mind wander back to that dark place – the place I have worked so hard to shut out. But I can't help it. *It wasn't my fucking fault. Stop BLAMING ME.*

The corners of my eyes begin to twitch and I know what

this means. I have at most thirty seconds before the tears appear. *I cannot cry. Not here. Not in front of Asher.*

"Fine, Ethan," I say tersely, snatching my towel off the chair. I can feel his words in my head telling me to cover myself, but I refuse. It's the only bit of rebellion I can muster.

I'm five steps away from the lounge chair when I hear Leo say, "Dude, leave your sister alone. Hasn't she been through enough?"

Well, damn. If I hadn't been on the brink of losing it before, I sure am now.

Three years. It had been three years since the incident, but it still trailed me like a stench I couldn't shake. Hearing Leo, one of Ethan's friends whom I rarely interact with, say *"hasn't she been through enough,"* told me everyone still remembered.

And here I was, thinking the world had moved past my trauma. Seems I was wrong. *Broken and helpless* – that's what they still thought of me. And dammit if they weren't fucking right.

CHAPTER 3

Asher

I FIND her in her room packing, and I can tell by the red splotches around her eyes she's been crying. *Fucking Ethan.* As commanded, she's no longer wearing the red bikini. Instead, she's donning jean shorts, a white tank top and wet hair from what I assume was a shower. I doubt she was expecting anyone to come check on her judging by the fact I can tell she's not wearing a bra, and the outline of her hard nipples against the thin cotton material of her tank has me more aroused than it should. *Though I'm not surprised.*

I rap my knuckles gently against the doorframe, wondering why she left the door open in the first place. I've decided I've waited long enough to suss out if she has any reciprocal interest in me. I've been harboring these feelings, this infatuation I have with her, for years now and it is finally time to make a move.

Panic washes over her face as her eyes settle on me, and she instantly looks away.

"Hey," she says, turning sideways. I know she's pretending to be busy to prevent me from seeing her tear-stained cheeks.

"Are you coming to the party tomorrow?" I ask.

She stuffs a few more things into a duffle bag. "If Ethan will allow it."

"If it were up to Ethan, I don't think you would be allowed to leave this house."

That was the wrong thing to say.

But mercifully, she laughs. "I know."

"Well, I hope you come," I say. "When do you leave for this camp?"

"This Sunday. My flight's at ten am."

"Is your mom flying with you?"

Wrong thing to say again.

She shakes her head. "No," she says softly. "My parents won't be back from Santa Barbara by the time I have to leave for the airport and I don't think my mom is well enough to make the trip anyway." I can hear the pain in her voice as she tells me this.

It occurs to me how uncomfortable she looks as I stand here, leaning against the door. I catch myself clenching my jaw as I study the brown and purple bruise on her arm, the circumference concerningly large to have come from an equally matched opponent. But it's the pink welt I know she has on her stomach that's sending me over the edge. If Ethan weren't such a good friend, I would have beaten his fucking ass into an unrecognizable pulp.

Wyatt is the only person who knows about the crush I've had on Addison since high school. He also knows what I did to that piece of shit Connor three years ago. I doubt Leo knows, although he might suspect I have a thing for her. According to Wyatt, it's obvious to anyone who has a pair of eyes. Thank god Leo and Ethan are both two grades ahead and blinded by their own egos. It's easier to hide the crush you have on your good friend's little sister when he's away at college and not around to see you shamelessly staring at her each time she passes you in the hallway.

Her red bikini today was reckless, and I'm sure she wore it

to get a rise out of Ethan – the flame of his temper is easy to stoke. I didn't like her wearing such a skimpy bikini either but not for the same reason as Ethan. When she walked outside and I watched the jaws of both Leo and Wyatt drop low enough to choke themselves on pool water, it took all my effort not to run over to her and cover her with my towel out of jealousy.

I'll be fucking dead before I allow another guy to see that much of her body again. The thought of her wearing that red bikini out in public?

No, it simply can't happen.

Before I can stop myself, I bend down to pick up the tousled heap of red strings now lying on the floor.

"What are you doing?" she asks, her eyes snapping to my hand.

"Taking this."

"Why?"

"So you can't wear it again."

"Did Ethan send you in here?"

"I don't think Ethan would let me so much as put a big toe in your bedroom."

"Then why are you taking my bathing suit? You have a thing for wearing women's clothing or something?"

I smirk. "As long as you're not the one wearing it."

"Why can't I wear it?"

In the moment, I can't think of anything witty to say, so I settle on, "You're not allowed."

"I'm not *allowed?*"

"Correct."

"Says who?"

"Says me. *I* won't allow it."

"Why?"

I close the distance between us until I'm standing near enough to feel her breath on my skin. She's forced to crane her neck backward to look up at me and I grin.

"You ask a lot of questions."

"Because you're not giving me any answers. What if I want to wear it to the party tomorrow?"

"Like hell you will." I'm smiling as I say this but I'm not trying to be funny and I love how venomous her eyes become as she glares at me.

"You *can't* wear it to the party tomorrow," I say, tilting her chin upward with my forefinger, "because I don't want to see you wearing this again unless I'm untying the strings with my teeth. And that can't exactly happen in front of an audience, can it?"

I give her a wicked smirk and watch the shock in her eyes transform into what I swear looks like a challenge. At least I got her thinking about something other than her asshole brother for a minute.

I turn to walk out of her room, and I almost make it when I hear, "Unless that's your thing."

I spin back around, confused.

"An audience," she clarifies with a mischievous upward curl of her lips.

"Oh," I say with calm realization, pinning her with my gaze. "I'm sorry to disappoint you, sweetheart, but I don't share."

CHAPTER 4

Addison

THANK *god they are finally here.* I bound down the stairs to open the front door for my friends Mira and Violet, who were too polite to barge in like the rest of the heathens now destroying my backyard. In no world would I have gone down to this party without reinforcements. Who would I talk to – the girls who were too popular in high school to befriend me but happy to gawk at me with pity after the incident happened? *I think not.*

Waiting in the confines of my room until my friends arrived was a much safer option. Besides, I'm sure everyone here is older by at least three years so I wouldn't exactly blend in with the crowd of beer-guzzling college kids. *Not yet at least.*

I open the door to find a wide-eyed Mira and a nervous Violet practically huddled together on my doorstep, clinging to each other for moral support.

"The noise from the street is crazy, Addison. How many people are here?" Violet stammers.

"No idea," I respond, ushering them inside. Maybe I was used to the sound of blaring music at this point, having spent my entire life as an unfortunate casualty in Ethan's quest to lose all ability to hear.

"What do you want to drink?" I ask as our strength-in-numbers cluster shuffles into the kitchen – handles of alcohol lining every inch of the counter. As soon as my parents left for Santa Barbara this morning, Ethan and his friends wasted no time *decorating*.

"What do you have?" Mira asks, her voice giddy, as if there weren't a full liquor cabinet on display in front of her. I flash her a look of judgment. She is far too excited for this night. But then again, we don't get out much. I wouldn't exactly call our small friend group a rabble of social butterflies. Swiping a bottle or two of rosé from our parents' wine racks when we have sleepovers was more our speed; however, the night we discovered tequila was a shit show. I'm pretty sure we decided to stress test whether we were attracted to the same sex that night, although none of us could really remember the next day. It's hard to conjure details when you're puking your guts up for hours.

"Well, we have all this," I motion to the supermarket liquor aisle that's currently our kitchen. "We also have beer, but the kegs are outside, there are spiked seltzers in the fridge, and I'm sure we have wine around here somewhere."

"Oooo, the *claw*," Mira says with a growl and accompanying hand gesture. *Jesus we are a hopeless bunch.*

"Oh! How about I make margaritas?" I offer.

Violet perks up at the mention of something familiar. "Yes," she agrees.

"K, you guys get the limes out of the fridge and find the tequila. I'll look for the pitcher and agave."

"Agave?" Violet asks.

"Violet, have you never had a margarita before?" Mira chides.

"It's a natural sweetener," I offer, shooting Mira a look. "I only know this because my mom refuses to eat refined sugar."

"I still don't know what you're talking about but whatever, just make it taste good," she says. I watch Violet pick up a random handle of alcohol off the counter, sniff it, and immediately gag. *Naturals. Making friends at college will be a walk in the park for us.*

I make my way to the pantry, and a twinge of sorrow flitters across my mind. College – two months away from the rest of our lives. I wonder if we will keep in touch when we all go our separate ways. I should have gone to Stanford with Mira. At least then I wouldn't be…

A deep voice cuts through my thoughts. "Looking for something?"

"Jesus," I jump, whirling to face the familiar sight of Asher leaning against a doorframe. His grin is even more smug than I remember.

"What is it with you and appearing out of thin air?"

"Your friends told me you were lost in the pantry."

"Oh, did they now?"

"They said you were lost trying to find your prince charming and, well, here I am." He flashes me a toothy smile.

"Wow. Lucky me. In that case, *prince*, fetch me my pitcher," I say as I motion upward.

He saunters toward me, his tanned skin dewy with the sheen of perspiration. The smell of outside air, mixed with tobacco and leather from his cologne, encases me, and I resist the urge to close my eyes as I inhale. He's standing so close now, I could press my palms against his chest and lean my head between them to hear his heartbeat.

"As you wish, princess," his deep, raspy voice more melodic than any symphony.

My gaze follows his arm upward in a fruitless attempt to track his hand, the sleeve of his T-shirt brushing my ear as he stretches to reach above me.

"This one?" he asks, bringing down a colorful acrylic pitcher.

"That'll do." I wonder if he can tell my flirtatious banter needs practice.

"Not so fast, princess," his words thick like honey as he dangles the pitcher out of my reach. "Where's my thank you?"

My brow furrows on instinct. "Um, *thank you*," I say snidely.

"I don't think so. Try again, sweetheart," his amusement dripping with wicked intentions.

I flash him my best saccharine-sweet smile. "Thank you, your highness."

He throws his head back with a bellowing laugh.

"That was terrible," he cackles.

Sobriety is not my friend right now but *fuck it.*

My fingers grab the nape of his neck and I pull, half trying to tug myself upward and half trying to yank him down. Our lips collide somewhere in the middle, and I can tell by the way he stumbles forward, he's as shocked as I am. I allow myself only a half-second to savor his perfect lips before panic takes over and forces me to push away.

I just kissed Asher Aves.

Every inch of my body is pulsing, and he scans my eyes, searching for an answer.

I'm sorry, I don't know why I did that, I want to say but stop myself.

"Is that better, prince?" I muster.

"Addison, did you find the pitcher or wh… ," Mira gasps. We both whip our heads in her direction to see Mira gaping at us. *Get the fuck out of here!* my expression screams at her, and she practically runs away.

A bemused chuckle escapes Asher's lips at Mira's juvenile bashfulness. "I think your friends are looking for you," he says with unnerving calm, turning back toward me.

I swallow my disappointment and take the pitcher. "I promised them margaritas," I sigh with annoyance as I brush past him.

The force of his pull catches me off guard and I stumble backward into his broad chest. He leans down to whisper in my ear, his cheek caressing mine as our faces touch.

"Don't kiss anyone else tonight, *princess*, because I'm not done with that pretty little mouth of yours."

He saunters away, throwing a casual smirk over his shoulder that leaves me speechless.

———

"What was *that?!*" Mira shrieks as I return to the kitchen.

"I think I'm hallucinating," I say and blink my eyes hard to clear my vision. I swear a blurry haze has settled around me, lifting me off my feet like a thick fog, and I'm not sure I can feel the ground anymore.

"No, what I saw was very much real," she squeals. "You were just making out with one of the hottest boys to ever graduate from our high school. Asher Aves is a legend."

"Oh my god," Mira squeals again. "AND you're both at Harvard now. Oh my god, Addison! Does he like you? Do you like him? Obviously you like him, right? I mean, who wouldn't? Just *look* at him."

"Maybe you won't go to college a virgin after all," Violet says dryly. How Violet has managed to lose her virginity and I haven't is baffling. Then again, given my crippling anxiety and neuroses, maybe not *that* surprising.

"I honestly don't know what's going on," I stutter. "It's like he started flirting with me out of the blue and now we're kissing in my pantry. Am I giving off a vibe or something?"

"Honey, you're always giving off a vibe," Violet grumbles, like it's the dumbest thing I've ever said.

"But no one has been into my brand of vibe before," I stutter. "Or at least not like this."

"That's because you hate everyone, Addison. I mean, face it, you're not the most approachable person. I'm even surprised you still hang out with us," Mira says. I can't tell if she's joking or not.

"I don't *hate* everyone."

The look on Mira's face says otherwise.

"Okay, fine, I'm *annoyed* by *almost* everyone. But it's because they're all fucking idiots, and I'd rather run a cheese grater over my skin than hear them talk. Not you two though."

Mira is giving me a look that says *I told you so.*

"Ugh," I sulk. "I am not excited about Harvard."

"Maybe that tall drink of water will change your mind!"

I laugh at Mira's optimism. "You're incorrigible, Mira."

"Speaking of tall drink," Violet cuts in. "Are we making margaritas or not?"

Right, the pitcher.

I begin slicing limes, but I'm so intensely focused on the interaction I just had with Asher, I lose track of what I'm doing.

"Fuck," I hiss, blood quickly seeping from the fresh cut as I clamp down on it with a paper towel.

"We're making margaritas, not Bloody Marys," Violet jabs.

"What happened?" Mira asks with concern.

"Cut myself. Can you finish these? I need to get a Band-Aid. You know how to make them, right?"

"Addison, I've *had* a margarita before. *Of course* I know how to make them. Have some faith," Mira assures me.

I doubt Mira has had so much as a sip of margarita before but I'm too worried about my wound to dole out instructions. She'll figure it out.

It takes me longer than expected to find a suitably sized

Band-Aid but thankfully when I get back, Mira presents me with a freshly made cup of witches' brew.

"Jesus, Mira, this is *awful*," I gag, nearly spitting out my sip. Turns out, book smarts do not equate to common sense.

"Is it?" she shrugs, taking a gulp. "I think it tastes good."

"Let me try," Violet says, taking a sip and then immediately spitting it back into the cup. "Good god, Mira. This is undrinkable. Did you put the entire bottle of tequila in the pitcher?"

Mira gives us a devilish grin. "Of course not, don't be silly."

Yep, she definitely did.

"Did you even put lime juice in here or did you just wave a lime over the pitcher hoping everything would turn out for the best?" I say sarcastically.

"Addison, don't be so dramatic," Mira laughs with an eye roll. "Keep drinking and it will start to taste better."

"If by taste better, you mean cause us to lose all ability to taste anything at all because we're blackout drunk, then sure, sounds like a solid plan."

Violet sets her cup down and crosses her arms in disgust.

I fish out an alcoholic seltzer from the fridge and hand it to Violet, opting to power through the monstrosity of a cocktail in my hand. If I'm going to subject myself to a party full of my brother's friends, I could use the extra dose of liquid courage.

"Let's go outside," I say. Mira bounces behind me, followed by a reluctant Violet.

Time to brave the elements.

CHAPTER 5

Addison

"ADDISON!" Mira shouts, her voice outrageously loud although she thinks she's being discreet. "Your dark angel is walking over here!"

I shoot her a look to keep it together, but she doubles over laughing.

Lush.

"You make me a drink?" he rasps, sitting down next to me.

"Do I look like your servant?"

"You look like you enjoy doing as you're told," he mutters into my ear and his warm breath against my neck sends a dangerous shiver down my spine.

Before I can stop him, the cup I was loosely clutching in my hands finds its way to his lips.

I watch him swallow, anticipating his reaction.

"Jesus, Addison, there's like a handle of tequila in here."

I laugh at his exaggeration but he doesn't seem to find it funny.

"I didn't make them! Mira did!"

He looks at me and then the remaining contents of the cup. "Was this full when you started?"

"About."

"You're not drinking any more of this," he grumbles as he stands.

I watch him disappear back into the crowd, and my mind can't sort through what just happened. *Is he genuinely upset or am I just not used to his dry sense of humor?*

"Should we go swimming?" Mira asks with the kind of manic enthusiasm only an intoxicated person could summon. I look down at her cup, my eyes widening when I see that she's drained it. She's in no condition to splash around in a kiddie pool, let alone jump into a body of water rimmed with concrete.

"Absolutely not," I have the wherewithal to say.

"YES! Let's go!"

Mira doesn't even hesitate, and ten seconds later, the smack of her fully-clothed body landing in the deep end of the pool can be heard by everyone within a five-mile radius.

Fuck. I know I have to jump in after her.

"Cannonball!" some drunk guy shouts before the tidal wave of his splash threatens to drown me. At least I'm not alone in this mess.

Seconds later, half the party is in the pool, and I'm fighting for my life among the hordes of splashing bodies. Finally, I make it to Mira who's flopping around without a care in the world. *Maybe this isn't so bad after all.*

"What the fuck are you doing?"

Shit. Ethan.

I look up to see his menacing frame now towering above me.

He is pissed.

He crouches down into a low squat, which can only mean he's a heartbeat away from yanking me out of the pool by my hair.

"The pool's going to be fucking trashed now, Addison, and Mom and Dad are going to lose their minds," he hisses.

His eyes blaze with fury. "I'm going to throttle you across this lawn when you get out."

Mira swims over, her strokes sloppy, as she reaches for the ledge and eyes Ethan with a look of drunk contempt.

"Addison, why is your brother such a…"

Fuuuuuuuck.

Puke.

Everywhere.

I watch Ethan's eyes go wide with horror as screams erupt and Mira's projectile puke spews from her mouth like an erupting volcano. I don't bother to see if chunks of vomit made it into the water, I know they have.

Bodies scatter like it's the zombie apocalypse, and I watch with dread as Ethan looks down at the putrid waste now covering his bare feet. *His flip-flop wearing, bare feet.* I can hear his string of curse words well after he's stormed off to presumably find a hose. I know my window of opportunity to get Mira out of here is now, lest she suffer even more humiliation.

"Mira, let's move over to the ladder and get out," I say as I tread water behind her.

"I'm so sorry, Addison," she weeps.

"It happens to everyone, Mira, it's not a big deal."

"But your *pool*."

"The pool will be fine." *Lord knows Ethan's friends have puked in it before. Hell, probably even Ethan himself.*

Mira struggles with her grip on the slippery ladder and just when I think I'm going to have to add lifeguard to list of life experiences, Mira floats effortlessly upward.

Asher sets her upright on the wet concrete and extends a hand down to me, which I gladly accept. I'm aware of how heavy my soaked clothes feel, clinging to my wet body, as I scramble up the ladder with Asher's aid.

Violet wastes no time and rushes in with a towel, shrouding Mira's shoulders as she bows her head in defeat.

The two of them scurry off, heading back inside the house, which leaves me completely exposed to the gaping stares and laughter of onlookers. I risk a glance down at myself and decide today is not the day to enter a wet T-shirt contest. I run inside, chasing Violet and Mira.

Violet has already collected both their purses and is two steps away from the front door when I reach them.

"V, you can't drive. You've been drinking."

"No, Addison, you and Mira were drinking, I wasn't."

"But I gave you a…"

"I didn't drink it. One of us has to stay sober, remember?"

I did remember the pact we made ages ago, vowing to always designate a sober chaperone at parties to make sure everyone in our group returned home safely. Hardly anyone invited us to any parties, of course, but Violet always had a knack for remembering details.

"Text us when you get to Johns Hopkins, Addison," Violet says with a grim look on her face.

Right. My flight.

"I will," I promise.

"I would hug you, but you're covered in puke. Where's Mira?" Violet whips around.

Mira, already halfway down the block, looks like a walking extra-terrestrial from the movies. "I have to go," Violet shouts over her shoulder as she chases down a barefoot Mira.

"Text me when you get home," I yell before shutting the front door.

I hear Ethan before I see him.

"Addison!" Ethan's voice booms down the hall. "Get the fuck back out there and clean up that shit. I said you and your friends were allowed to come on one condition, which was to stay out of the way. That was the OPPOSITE of staying out of the way."

"I'll clean it up before I leave tomorrow, Ethan. It's dark outside and I won't be able to see all the damage."

Our shouting begins to draw an audience. *Fabulous.*

"Now, Addison!" he screams, yanking my wrist to follow him back outside.

"Ethan, STOP!" I protest, literally digging in my heels. "I'm freezing and covered in puke!"

"NOW!"

"ETHAN, LET GO OF ME!"

"Enough, Ethan!" I hear Asher's voice cut through our squabble before I can register his presence. Ethan drops my wrist but the fight in his eyes still rages.

"I said, *that's enough*," Asher says. His tone is low and threatening, as he steps inches from Ethan's face. I feel like I'm watching a staring contest. Fortunately for me, Ethan blinks.

"*Fine*, but don't think I'm driving your fucking ass to the airport tomorrow morning, Addison," he hisses.

He turns to walk away but not before hammering one last nail in my coffin: "And change your clothes. You look like a drowned rat, and I can see your fucking tits."

I cover myself instinctually, ashamed, as he parts his way through the crowd of spectators.

I hurry back upstairs to the safety of my room, locking the door. The night wasn't supposed to end like this – covered in puke and humiliated. But Mira was right about one thing.

Asher is a spectacular dark angel.

CHAPTER 6

Addison

MY EYES DART open at an unmistakable crashing sound, followed by the cackle of female laughter emanating through the wall I share with Ethan's bedroom. How I managed to doze off despite all the noise downstairs is beyond me.

I can tell by the pitch of the female's voice it's Clara – Ethan's former high school girlfriend turned friends with benefits when they both are home from college.

My god, Ethan was out of his mind tonight. His proclivity for a certain white powder has seemingly gotten worse. He's not entirely to blame. It's practically a rite of passage if you attend one of the private high schools in Los Angeles. Access is rampant, making experimentation inevitable, although drugs have never been my thing.

No, Ethan and I are very different when it comes to our social desires. Sometimes I wonder if the incident with Connor never happened, would I still be this way – reclusive and critical? Or would I have grown up more jovial and care-free like Ethan? It certainly would make my life easier if I could be more like him.

Two a.m.

I don't hear any more noise outside, but just as I flop

down against my pillow, content to go back to sleep, the moaning starts.

Well, if I wasn't awake before, I'm awake now.

The high-pitched pants followed by guttural grunts are so loud, I half expect to sit up and see them writhing on the floor in front of me.

No, no, no. I will not bear witness to the sound of my brother ejaculating. I flip my covers off quickly but remind myself to tiptoe so I don't alert my security guard of a brother that his prisoner has escaped.

Downstairs is eerily quiet, save for the ticking of my mother's heirloom wall clock in the kitchen. I assumed the party had died down but didn't realize it was over. Male bodies, presumably my brother's friends, were strewn about – the lucky ones sleeping on couches and chairs, the unlucky ones left to curl up with a blanket and pillow on the floor.

Oh my god. Even with reduced visibility in the dark, I can tell the kitchen is a complete *disaster.*

From the corner of my eye, I see a shadowy figure emerge and am instantly transported back to the girls' bathroom three years ago. Panic floods my veins, and my heart threatens to burst through my ribcage. I start to bolt but my mind is racing faster than my limbs, now gone clumsy with fear, and my forearm knocks right into my water glass as I turn to run. A split second later, I hear it shatter against the floor.

Shit.

Shit. Shit. Shit.

"Don't move."

And why does it have to be him?

I know that deep voice by now. Glass is scattered all around my feet, but I plant them firmly against the tile to maintain my balance. The last thing I need is an emergency room visit tonight.

Asher, the emerging shadowy figure responsible for my

fright, crouches down and begins gingerly gathering the broken glass into a neat pile with a dishrag.

"Quite the night you're having, princess," he says smugly.

"And where would I be without my knight in shining armor, ready to save me from myself?" I scoff.

"Careful," he says with delicate firmness, still crouching at my feet. "I'm almost done."

"Why are you still awake?" I ask.

"Waiting to save you, of course."

I huff a laugh. "No, seriously. Everyone else appears to be passed out."

He shrugs as he stands. He's managed to sweep all the glass onto a paper plate and walks over to the waste bin to discard my handiwork.

"Couldn't sleep so I started cleaning."

"Doesn't look like you got very far," I tease.

"Admittedly, cleaning is not one of my many talents."

I cock a brow. "*Many* talents?"

"Too many to count, really."

"Like what?"

"Oh, well let's see. Fetching pitchers, rescuing drunk girls from pools, stopping drunk girls from slicing their feet open on broken glass…"

"I'm not drunk," I cut in.

"No?" He leans forward against the countertop, placing a hand on either side of me as he studies my pupils. I resist the urge to run my fingers up his biceps. "What would you call yourself then?"

"You startled me is all. I didn't think anyone was awake." I cross my arms in a demure stance and rest my index finger against my bottom lip, parting it slightly.

"Disappointed?"

I roll my eyes at his bravado. *He knows I'm not disappointed.*

"If you're not drunk, then tell me what I said to you before your puking friend cock-blocked me."

"*Mira?* When did she cock-block you?"

"When we were in the pantry. When I told you I was far from done with your pretty little mouth."

Oh, right. I give him a knowing grin.

"You said not to kiss anyone else."

"And?"

"And you would be pleased to know that between dodging chunks of puke and getting screamed at by Ethan, I wasn't able to find the time to ensnare another suitor."

He shakes his head, looking off to the side, as the muscles in his jaw twitch.

"Is he always like that with you?"

"He didn't used to be. It's definitely gotten worse after…"

I swallow, stopping myself as I glance down at my thankfully cut-free feet.

"Yeah, well, that's going to stop."

I doubt anyone can put a stop to Ethan's behavior. But after tonight's showdown, maybe Ethan does have an Achilles heel.

"Is that what you think you did?" he asks, changing the subject. "Ensnare me?"

I chuckle. "Was it not?"

"I'm pretty sure I came into the pantry of my own free will."

"But I'm the one who kissed you."

"I guess my telepathic insemination worked."

"Your what now?"

He drops his head in laughter, and the hair on the top of his head skims my cotton nightshirt.

I'm smiling, watching his trapezius muscles quiver, as he abruptly raises his head, his lips mere inches from mine, and schools his face into serious intensity.

"Kiss me again, princess."

My heart begins racing and I allow my hand to wander over to his cheek, skimming his smooth lips with my thumb. Our eyes lock and he's so close, I can feel the breath he takes in the second before his mouth presses against mine.

Heat washes over every inch of me, threatening to burn me from the inside out. I'm vaguely aware of the countertop jutting into my back as he presses his chest against mine.

But all I can feel is the sensation of our tongues touching, the taste of our mouths together, his fingertips digging into the back of my head to pull my mouth in closer, the throb in between my legs begging for attention. Everything else has gone numb.

I don't know where I get the confidence, but I start moving his other hand down my abdomen. As soon as his fingers meet flesh, he withdraws.

"Let's go upstairs," he whispers against my earlobe. His arms move too fast for me to register the sweeping motion that follows.

I shoot him a look that says *this is completely unnecessary* but he only smirks at me with delight. I could object to being carried but *why would I?*

Upstairs, he gently lays me down on the bed, then turns back to quietly shut my door. I watch him stride across my room, all six-foot something of him, and pray he can't detect my nerves. The bed creaks as he slowly positions himself on top of me.

"Is this okay?" he asks, his voice barely a whisper. Ethan and Clara are audibly going at it one room over, but the precaution still feels necessary.

I nod, even though I feel on the verge of hyperventilating.

His lips graze mine with a soft, careful kiss as his fingertips delicately tuck a loose strand of hair behind my ear.

"You're so tense, princess."

"I know," I breathe, my eyes catching his before blinking away. *Why did I say that?*

"What's wrong?" His lips feather against my jawline,

resting against my scar, before moving down my neck with a trail of unhurried kisses.

"Nothing. I just…"

Don't say it, don't say it, don't say it.

"Just what?" His kisses find their way to the thin skin of my throat, and my entire body shivers.

"I haven't done this before."

"I know," he whispers.

How did he know? He's at my collarbone and the throbbing need between my legs is screaming at me to shut my mouth.

"And I don't have any condoms."

Well, that stopped him.

"Addison."

He says my name with firm resolve.

"I don't plan on fucking you tonight."

Embarrassment coils in my stomach.

"Oh," I say meekly, the word catching in my throat.

"I'm not fucking you when your brother is within earshot of your orgasm," he explains.

My embarrassment begins to uncoil.

"When are you back from nerd camp?" he whispers.

"The end of July."

"Seriously?" The shock plastered across his face draws a smile from my lips.

"Seriously."

"Fuck," I hear him mutter.

"Then I can't let you leave without tasting you first."

His hand glides up my torso to remove my shirt, and I arch my back. A quick tug has it over my head and the nipples of my now-bare breasts harden under the traces of his thumbs.

"My god," he whispers before I feel his tongue swirl around my left nipple. His other hand palms the entirety of my right breast, ensuring neither side is neglected.

A silent gasp escapes my lips as his mouth trails the length of my abdomen, kissing me inch by inch until I'm writhing with anticipation. My thin cotton shorts and panties don't put up a fight as he pulls them down over my hips and tosses both to the floor. Sitting back on his heels, I watch him take in the entirety of my nakedness, eyes scanning me with intention until he lands on the swollen pink flesh between my legs. My breathing has become choppy as I await his next move.

He hinges forward and grabs the pillow next to my head, handing it to me. I must have furrowed my brow in confusion because he lowers himself next to my ear with a smug grin on his face and whispers, "I'm about to eat your pussy like it's my death row meal, Addison. I doubt you want to wake the entire house when you scream."

Before I can process the warning, my thighs are spread open like heavy pages of a thick book, and air tickles me in places it never has before. Hot breath hovers at my entrance as his lips kiss the length of me. A tingly sensation fills my crevices, and a pulsating thunder swells within my core. The anticipation of what his tongue will feel like when it pushes me apart threatens to be my undoing, and I clutch the pillow in my arms even tighter.

A gasp slips from my lips as the tip of his warm tongue parts me, then drags up my slit. I barely get the pillow over my face in time as it starts to run circles around my clit, slowly at first then faster with intention.

My back arches in delight as I feel his tongue drag back down to my opening. Despite my best efforts, I moan when I feel the full girth of his tongue dip in and out of me. Pain from his fingertips digging into my supple skin blooms across my outer thighs as he yanks me in closer. The gift of his mouth is everything, yet it's still not enough. I want, *I need*, more of him.

Two thick fingers slide inside me, and I erupt at the pressure. I want to scream his name but don't, unsure of the pillow's efficacy in such uncharted territory. I open-mouth, silent scream instead as I grind myself against him mercilessly.

Even through the pillow, I can hear my wet arousal as his fingers pump in and out of me. My abdomen tightens and I can feel my release building. He's sucking my nub and finger-fucking me simultaneously and goddamn do I never want him to stop.

A strangled moan escapes into the muffled protection of the pillow as my orgasm crests, unleashing itself into his mouth as my chest heaves in satisfaction. A full-body shudder careens down my spine, and I quiver uncontrollably for five heartbeats until the stars I see behind my closed eyelids dim.

Breathe. I need to breathe but I can't remember how.

I try to steady myself, pulling the pillow off my flushed face. I feel him lap up one last mouthful of me and look down to see him swallow.

My head is dizzy and blank at the same time, maybe from the lack of oxygen while under the pillow. I watch him wipe his mouth on the back of his hand and I blink to see his face once again above mine, tucking my disheveled hair back into place. The way he looks at me is soft and caring, scanning my face with subtle concern. I didn't know someone with such a vicious reputation was capable of such tenderness.

"What are you thinking?" I ask, my heart still pounding against my chest.

He doesn't immediately answer, content to study me for a few more breaths.

"I'm thinking if I had it my way, Addison, you'd be my first, last, and only meal for the rest of my life."

CHAPTER 7

Asher

SHE'S FLUSTERED when I see her, confused as to why I am waiting outside of her room at seven a.m.

"Ready?" I ask, reaching over to take her suitcase and duffle bag.

"You don't have to drive me," she quietly protests. I give her a look that says *don't be ridiculous*. In no world would I let her get into a car with a stranger when her taste is still on my tongue.

She was so wet last night, but I knew she was still holding back. Next time I want her dripping and feral, wet enough to drown me. But there was no way either of us could reach full satiety with Ethan next door, even if he was preoccupied with Clara.

I waited until I was sure she was asleep to slip out. If Ethan caught us, he would undoubtedly take his rage out on her, and I wasn't ready to add murderer to the list of my accomplishments just yet. *Although I know I've already come close.*

I can tell she's a nervous flyer by the way she keeps zipping and unzipping her bag, checking compulsively for something she already knows is there. I reach over to take her hand, entwining my fingers in hers as I stroke soothing circles with my thumb. This seems to help, and she stills, gazing out the window at passing traffic.

Her skin glows against the soft morning light. The LA sky is still cloaked in light gray clouds from the marine layer, and only hints of sunshine peek through. I want to ask her how she gets away with being so beautiful, but I think conversation will just make her more nervous.

Finally, I can't help myself.

"So how many students go to this nerd camp?"

She chuckles. "I have no idea," she says, looking over at me.

"Where do you stay?"

"In the dorms."

"In a single?"

"God, I hope so."

I bring the back of her hand up to my mouth and kiss it before placing both of our hands back down on her thigh.

Dangerous.

Now I'm going to have to spend the rest of the drive resisting the urge to touch her.

"What is that tattoo on your leg?"

"You saw that?" I ask, delaying my answer. I'm not ready to talk about this, about the sigil I have tattooed in black ink on my upper thigh that symbolizes retribution and vengeance, but she's looking at me expectantly and I worry I'll upset her if I don't.

"You don't have to tell me if you don't want to," she says, sensing my hesitation.

"It's not that, it's just… complicated."

"Is it about an ex?"

I snort. "An ex-father, does that count?"

Well shit, now I've opened Pandora's box.

I can tell she doesn't know what to say so I offer her a partial truth. "My biological dad left my mom and I when I was young, and the tattoo is a reminder of sorts to keep going."

"Has anyone ever told you that you have very intense eyes?" she asks, mercifully changing the subject.

"Most people tell me I'm an asshole," I grin.

She contemplates my response. "Do you agree?"

"What do you think?"

"I think you very much like playing this character," she smirks, and I raise a brow in her direction.

I bring her hand to my lips again and plant a lingering kiss this time, looking at her through the sides of my eyes. I try to restrain my smile as I see her watching, holding her breath, and I find myself wishing I was driving her down to Mexico instead of the airport.

"Will you miss me?" I ask, baiting her.

"Parts of you, yes," she says with a wicked grin.

"You and your words, princess," I sigh as I pull into the airport departures lane.

She swings the door open, and I get out to take her bags from the trunk. There are so many things I want to say, *should say,* but all I manage is "I'll call you." I kiss her briefly on the lips, not because I'm in a rush, but because if I drag this out any longer, I'm going to toss her and her bags back into my G-Wagen and make a run for the border.

She gives me a shy smile and wave before disappearing into the terminal. The sinking feeling in the pit of my stomach threatens to pull me under.

A blaring ring from my car speakers shocks me back to reality.

Fuck, why is Ethan calling me?

"Morning, sunshine," I say. I am ninety-nine percent sure I know what this is about, and it's not to thank me for driving his baby sister to the airport.

"Where are you?" he growls.

"Driving."

"Driving where?"

"Home?"

"Stop fucking with me, Asher, home from where?"

It's too early for another one of his tirades.

"You want to tell me why my sister's room smells like you?"

"Smells like me?" I feign. "That's a strange thing to say."

"Why does my sister's room smell like that fucking cologne you always wear? Is it because you *fucked* her last night?" he seethes.

"I helped her with her bags this morning, psycho!" *Not a total lie.*

"And then you drove her to the airport?"

"I was just trying to be nice, Ethan."

"Bullshit, Asher. You never do something *just to be nice.* You don't think I see the way you look at her? The way you've always looked at her? It's obvious you have a thing for my sister."

Is it? I wonder.

"So, what?" Ethan continues. "You wait until I'm out of the picture, until I've graduated to make your move because you know I won't be physically at Harvard to beat your ass when you break her heart? Has that been your plan all along?"

It was, but I wasn't going to admit it.

"For fuck's sake Ethan, *calm down!* I felt bad for her after you reamed her out in front of the entire party."

"Because she puked in the pool?"

"Because *her friend* puked in the pool."

"Shit, I don't remember."

"Maybe chill out on the drugs, bro."

"Like you're one to talk, Aves."

He did have a point.

"Anyway, how about a 'thank you, Asher, for driving my sister to the airport this morning after I was a raging dick to her last night and humiliated her in front of everyone.'"

"Ughhhhh," he groans loudly. "What am I going to do when she starts school in the fall? You know what she's been through. I'm worried Harvard will eat her alive. You'll watch out for her, won't you? I don't want her getting involved with any dickhead frat guys."

"Like me?" I ask, half joking.

"Definitely not you. Jesus Christ, Asher, my sister wouldn't know what to do with you. She's so innocent and pure and you're…," he pauses.

"Not?"

"You know it's true, Asher. You're too smart for your own good. Besides, aren't you with Chloe? She's more your speed."

I scoff. "No, and she's the opposite of my speed. She's fun but she's…"

"Crazy." Ethan finishes my sentence for me.

"Yes, and not in a good way."

"You book your Hamptons flight yet for July Fourth?"

"I need to do it today," I remember.

"Well, get on it. I've already got parties lined up. Wyatt and Leo are flying into the city on the second, and we'll drive up on the third with Jaxon."

"Yeah, I just need to figure out when my G-Wagen will arrive. I'm going to ship it back east for school. Might have to fly in a few days early."

"You and that fucking G-Wagen of yours. Whatever, just be there, okay? I know how you like to abruptly change course at the last minute."

I roll my eyes but I know he's not wrong.

"Get back here and help me clean up this shit, will you? My house is fucking trashed."

"Fine," I agree. There is nothing in the world I hate more than cleaning.

"Oh, and Asher," Ethan interjects before I can hang up the call. "I'm serious. You fuck my sister and you die."

The line goes quiet, and I switch my audio back to a playlist I made this morning while waiting for Addison to emerge. The marine layer shrouding LA has yet to burn off and its melancholy gray is the perfect reflection of my mental state. I curse under my breath, painfully aware that Addison's scent still lingers on my fingers. I know I won't be able to control myself once the barriers of proximity and Ethan's surveillance no longer stand in my way.

I'm a dead man walking.

CHAPTER 8

Addison

I'VE NEVER BEEN SO tired. My only saving grace is I don't have to share this tiny hole of a dorm room with anyone else for the next six weeks.

I promised my mom I'd call her the moment I was settled, but between navigating a taxi and an unfamiliar campus with an oversized suitcase, I'm exhausted. She'll have to make do with a text.

I unzip my monstrosity of a bag to fish out my sheets. I had tried to nap on the plane. I even had the foresight to pack my pillow and blanket in my carry-on, but after last night, there was no way I could still my mind. Every five minutes the memory of him between my legs flashed into my mind and I'd snap awake, covered with goosebumps yet again.

He had been so smug and nonchalant this morning on the drive to the airport. I was grateful for the ride, but the way he held my hand made me wonder what the hell was going on between us. I'm so confused – *so, so confused* by the whole thing.

I can't get his eyes out of my head – sometimes dark green, sometimes hazel, with a glowing inner halo that blazes with copper flecks when it catches the sunlight.

How am I going to focus while I'm here? He said he would call, but will he? Does Ethan know? *God, I hope not.* Should I follow Asher on social media, or hold off?

I'm waging this war in my head when I notice the contents of my suitcase are not in the order I had packed them.

Did TSA go through my suitcase at the airport?

Frantically I start checking to see if anything is missing.

T-shirts, shorts, jeans, tanks, bras. WHERE ARE MY UNDERWEAR?

What the fuck? I had packed a boatload of undergarments so why do I only have four pairs of *period panties* in my suitcase?

Wait, hold on.

WHERE ARE MY GOOD BRAS?

I can remember at least five bras and double the number of panties I packed for this trip. And none of them are in this suitcase.

Am I wrong? Did I forget to pack them?

I'm about to call my mom to ask her to overnight me a package when my phone dings with an incoming text message.

Did you make it? from an unknown number.

Who is this?

Who do you think?

Truly no idea.

I'll give you a hint.

Seconds later the number sends a picture of my red bikini straps between a set of perfectly white teeth, top lip upturned in a snarl.

A giddy flush erupts in my stomach.

How did you get my number?

Don't worry about it.

A thought sparks in my mind.

Did you take the underwear out of my suitcase?

Three dots appear, and I'm ripe with anticipation.

I can't think of a reason why you would need lacy bras and panties at nerd camp.

Lord save me, I think to myself. And why the hell am I smiling like a deranged cat?

You really do have a thing for women's clothing, don't you? I type back.

Hmm, if you say so princess.

Well I'm going to buy more.

Don't.

But I like wearing them.

Three dots again.

I think you mean "I like wearing them for you and only you, Asher" and "You're right, I don't need them at nerd camp because I'm not going to wear them until I see you again."

Wow…

Aww, don't worry princess. I'll keep them safe for you.

Ok, presumptuous.

What is?

Assuming there will be a next time.

Won't there?

Before I can come up with a clever response, he sends another text that ends me.

That's what I thought.

CHAPTER 9

Addison

I LOOK up at the sterile white ceiling, and it takes precisely three blinks before I know I've made a colossal mistake. What was I thinking when I decided to spend six weeks across the country by myself attending a toned-down version of college… before actual college even starts? *Am I that much of a masochist?*

I suppose I'll also be alone when I start at Harvard but if I had stayed in LA, Asher and I might have spent more time together and perhaps more time would have transformed our one-night hookup into a relationship. Asher *could* have become my boyfriend over the summer. A significant other would certainly make starting college less intimidating.

Now that I'm here at Johns Hopkins, I know there's no chance of this happening. I don't get back to LA until the end of July and even if Asher is still around then, we wouldn't have time for a relationship to develop. I leave for Harvard two weeks later. *It was probably wishful thinking anyway.*

This is a disaster.

I can feel the panic rising in my throat, and my heart rate elevates.

"Practice your breathing," my therapist, Dr. Mindy, had reminded me before I left.

When I first received the news I was accepted into this program, I was elated. But as soon as I told my mom, the realization I would be away from her – from home, by myself – came crashing down. I had told my mom I wanted to drive over to Violet's house to tell her the exciting news in person. But in reality, I got in the Jeep I inherited from Ethan and made it four blocks before having a full-blown panic attack.

I've been hiding the return of my crippling anxiety from my family, especially my mom, for the last six months.

Despite the hours I've spent in therapy with Dr. Mindy since the incident with Connor happened, I always seem to regress to this place of fear and self-loathing.

I'm on the floor of the dorm room now, shaking as I curl my legs into my chest. One of the more annoying symptoms of these panic attacks is the loss of vision – I can barely see straight, and I'm supposed to check in for this program in less than an hour. Getting off the floor feels impossible.

Breathe in, hold your breath for four seconds, breathe out, slowly.

I should take an anti-anxiety pill but I hate relying on medication to get through these episodes. Needing medication seems to give power to the little voice in the back of my head – the one that likes to remind me I'm still weak, still not over what happened, still broken. I want to fight it, but I know everything this stupid little voice says is true.

I hear Dr. Mindy's words echoing in my mind: "It's not about being weak or not being weak. It's about getting back to neutral. It's about being able to enjoy your life, not simply survive it."

I try to unlock my phone to text Dr. Mindy, but my vision is so blurry, I can't see the screen.

Great, I guess I'm going to be morbidly late on my first day. What a wonderful first impression.

It's nearly eleven a.m., three hours after check-in, when I finally make it to the right building on campus and find the classroom. The man standing in the front of the room stops whatever he's saying and looks at me like I've surely taken a wrong turn.

"Can I help you?" he asks, annoyed at the interruption.

"I'm here for the summer pre-med research program. I'm Addison Blaise."

"Well, Ms. Blaise, you're late. Please take a seat," he extends an arm to the lecture seats in front of him and I've never been so mortified. I hardly allow a breath to escape my lips until his overview of the program ends forty-five minutes later.

Our lunch hour starts afterwards, and I'm eager to learn what I missed while in the throes of what I'm sure was the first of many panic attacks I'll suffer here this summer.

To my surprise, conversation over lunch is downright delightful. *These are my people.*

The other students are friendly and good-natured – most, like me, start college in the fall. There are a few older pre-med students. But all of us are shades of strange. I guess you'd have to be to want to do something like this over the summer instead of partying or backpacking around Europe.

I'm trying to discern what I missed this morning when a pair of bright blue eyes at the end of the table catches my attention.

He waves at me, and I immediately blush before having the wherewithal to wave back. Seconds later, he is striding toward me.

"Hi, I'm Gavin," he says, turning around a chair from a neighboring table. *He is far too handsome for this program.*

"Addison," I respond, extending my arm to offer a handshake.

"You were the girl who arrived late this morning, right?"

"That's me."

"Get lost?"

"Something like that."

"Are you already in school?"

"No, I start Harvard this fall."

A cocky smirk quirks at his lips.

"What about you?" I ask. It's not what I want to say. I want to ask him what's so funny about Harvard but I resist the urge to be combative. This program literally just started.

"Stanford."

"Oh, nice. I thought about going there."

"You got in?"

My brows furrow at his skepticism but I quickly coax my expression back to neutral.

"I did."

"Too bad you didn't go. We could have been classmates," he responds with an all-too-confident smile.

"So, I guess we're stuck here for the next six weeks together," he continues, his tone laced with flirtation.

"I guess we are," I smile. "Can you tell me what I missed this morning?"

He recounts the program overview while I admire the mop of shaggy, blonde hair adorning his head like a crown.

"After lunch, we head to the lab where we'll meet our PhD research teams," he says. "Maybe we'll get lucky and our lab stations will be close to each other."

He smiles, scooting in his chair.

"Maybe," I smile back. He's cute in a very boy-next-door sort of way. His playful banter is endearing and awkward, despite his shameless attempts at flirting, and I'm glad to have found a fellow cute nerd in the program.

Trouble.

CHAPTER 10
Addison

"HONESTLY, I really don't think the synthetic RNA will bind with the proteins," Gavin says. After two weeks and far too much time spent on campus, our little nerd group decided we should take a break from the dining halls and venture to an actual restaurant.

The four of us, myself, Gavin, Malik and Ava, had sniffed each other out within the first twenty-four hours and made an unspoken pact to stick together. *The cool nerds.* You can usually tell who is and isn't a cool nerd by the amount of eye contact. If someone can look you in the eye and carry on normal conversation, they're a keeper.

We are nearing the halfway point of the program, and the pressure we all feel to prove ourselves valuable is mounting.

"It makes sense in theory," Gavin continues a bit too loudly. "But in practice, I'm not sure it will work in an actual cellular environment."

We were all a little drunk at this point after an extended pregame at the dorms.

"Addison, I think your project is the most interesting," he adds.

"I mean, compared to yours, I think it has a better chance

of being successful," I say. "We still have a lot of data to process before we can even begin to draw any preliminary conclusions. It's definitely not going to be anywhere near wrapped up by the time this program is over, which is a bummer."

"That's research for you," Malik says. "Very long timelines."

"Guys, are we going out tonight?" Ava asks. "I think we should go to the club downtown my friend was telling me about – the one in the warehouse. She said they don't check IDs!"

I want to say it sounds super sketchy. But I hold my tongue, not wanting to be the rain cloud over Ava's enthusiasm.

"Does anyone have to be up early tomorrow?" Malik asks.

"Nope," Gavin confirms, as Ava and I shake our heads. "Let's do it!"

Despite his initial flirtation, Gavin has maintained a frustratingly platonic stance for the past three weeks. Maybe I'm not his type. Maybe girls aren't his type in general. Settling for friendship did, however, make things less complicated and awkward.

It definitely would get uncomfortable if we hooked up and made things weird for ourselves and our small friend group. Flirting without any expectations has been liberating in a way – a silently understood line neither of us would cross.

A few hours later, we're in line at the "club" – a generous description for what I would describe as an abandoned storage building teeming with grime and graffiti – and Ava was right. They didn't card us, or anyone for that matter. Maybe this is what underground clubs are like? I've never been to one and am a bit out of my element, but I try to go with the flow like I do this all the time back in LA.

Ava pulls my arm through the crowd as we make our way to the bar to order four tequila shots and four beers.

"So," Ava screams into my ear as we wait. "What's the deal with you and Gavin?"

"Nothing," I scream back, over the music. "We're just friends."

"He's interested," she yells, and I give her a look to say she couldn't be more wrong.

"It's true!" Ava yells emphatically. "You should make a move! He's too shy."

Shy? Are we talking about the same person here?

Gavin and Malik make their way behind us just in time to grab their drinks.

"Bottoms up!" Malik hoots as we all throw back our shots. I nearly spit out the piss-warm, rancid liquor claiming to be tequila. It's so bad I have to chug my beer to chase away the awful taste.

"Let's dance," Gavin commands, motioning to the dance floor. I must be drunk because I'm happy to follow, willing the pounding waves of sound to wash over my body, loosening the restrictive leash I typically keep on myself.

Maybe it's the tequila that has Gavin so unfurled. His arms have been banded around my waist most of the night, pulling me in closer as we grind wildly against each other to the thump of the music. His roaming hands keep finding their way down my hips and up the side of my ribcage, and I've felt his lips against the side of my neck multiple times.

It's approaching three a.m. when we get back to the dorms, and my rosy cheeks are flush with serotonin. Ava and Malik head toward their rooms, and I deliberately linger behind, convinced what Ava told me earlier about Gavin is true. His blatant show of affection felt like confirmation of his interest. *How could it not when our flesh was fused together on the dance floor for hours?*

My only regret of the evening so far is documenting our

debauchery on social media. I pray Ethan doesn't see the posts before they expire in twenty-four hours. I didn't do anything horrible, but going to an underground club isn't the kind of thing I want to flaunt in my brother's face. Most of the pictures were just our group having fun – sweaty bodies glued together on the dance floor, euphoria plastered across our faces – but I know he monitors my social media posts like a hawk.

"Will you get back to your room okay?" Gavin asks as we walk down the hall then pause at his room.

"Oh, you're going to bed?" I ask drunkenly, a bit surprised.

We continue to linger awkwardly in the hallway, slowly inching closer together, until I'm unable to control myself. I stand on my tiptoes to kiss him. For a moment, he kisses me back but abruptly pushes me away. In my drunken stupor, I stumble.

"I'm sorry," he says. "I just don't think this is a good idea."

"Okay…," I say, letting out an embarrassed laugh as I take another step backward.

"I'm sure I'm going to regret this but we're both really drunk right now. If this is going to happen, I think we should wait until the end of the program. Just so we don't make it weird, you know?"

"Yeah, I get it," I say. I'm staggering backward now, trying not to trip over my feet. "I'll see you tomorrow," I manage and turn around to walk toward my room. As soon as I hear his door shut, I bolt.

Oh my god, oh my god, that was so fucking horrible. I'm such an IDIOT. I should have NEVER listened to Ava.

I fumble with my key and finally get the latch to open, throwing my purse against the wall as I starfish down on my bed.

Fuck, the room is spinning.

My phone dings from across the room with a text.

Please don't let this be Ethan, I think, remembering LA is three hours behind Baltimore.

You seem to have forgotten what I told you.

I study the screen with confusion. *Why is Asher texting me?*

After the first week went by and he didn't call, I foolishly still felt hopeful. I rationalized it in my mind. Time moves differently for boys his age. Everyone knows the rule – three days before a boy will text you, so a phone call must take at least a week.

Then the DMs started: *How's nerd camp? I miss you baby. You're so beautiful. I can't wait to see you again princess.* Why was this guy sliding into my DMs but not calling me?

Just fucking pick up the phone! I wanted to scream. It didn't make any sense.

After the second week came and went, the anger set in, and I stopped responding to the DMs. Three weeks later, I felt heartbroken and stupid, even though I know I have no right. It was one night. *One night.* Obviously it was nothing more than a fling of convenience – the right place at the right time. Still, I couldn't help but feel hurt. I had gotten my hopes up. *So stupid.*

I blink again, convinced I've misread the screen – it must be Ethan and not Asher.

I scroll back through the text history, and *nope, it's Asher.*

Umm, hi? I text back, although my dexterity is questionable.

Who is he? he texts.

Who?

Don't play dumb.

I'm so confused, I respond.

Did you fuck him?

Fuck who?

THE FUCKING GUY IN YOUR SOCIAL MEDIA POSTS, ADDISON. Answer my fucking question, did you fuck him?

My head is spinning. Is he yelling at me? He's texting in all caps.

I can't tell if I'm feeling fear or annoyance or anger, so I respond with just two words:

Not yet.

Those unnerving three dots bounce around in my line of sight.

Finally he responds: *Let me remind you Addison, I do not share.*

You're an asshole. It's the lamest comeback of all time, but it's the only response my brain, sloppy and slow from a night of drinking, can think to say.

Keep fucking with me, Addison, and I'll show you how much of an asshole I can really be.

Is that a threat?

It's a promise, princess.

CHAPTER 11

Addison

"YOU GOING to be okay taking the bus by yourself?" Ava asks, pulling up to the station in the sensible hybrid SUV she borrowed from her older sister this summer.

"I'll be fine," I say, although my tone does not sound reassuring. "Seriously, it's only a four-hour trip, maybe less, and I'll sleep the whole way."

"Okay." Ava looks at me with uncertainty.

"Oh, and I took your advice and made a move on Gavin last night," I add as if it's an afterthought. Truthfully, I've been too embarrassed to admit my failure.

"And?!" she asks with glee.

I shake my head. "He was pretty much like 'thanks but no thanks' and went to bed."

"WHAT?! Are you serious?!"

"Yep, I feel like a complete fool. I kissed him in the hallway outside his room last night and then he pushed me away. So, yeah, I guess that's a no for me," I say, trying to play off how dejected and ashamed I feel.

"Whoa, what a dick," Ava says. "I'm shocked. He always talks about how hot you are. Malik said he talks about trying to get with you all the time."

"Well, I guess he was all talk," I say, disappointed by Ava's erroneous information.

"That sucks, I'm sorry. Dang, is it going to be awkward now?" Ava asks.

"Probably," I say matter-of-factly and shrug. "What can you do?"

"Fucking men," she laments. "Text me when you get to New York City so I know you made it, okay?"

I nod and board the bus. *Fucking men, indeed.*

Resisting the urge to text Asher back last night to ignite a full-on war took all my strength. I tossed in bed for what felt like hours, checking my phone every fifteen minutes to see if he had texted again – *apologized.* Nothing. Not a fucking word.

I should have called him out on his lie – his promise to call me. I don't know why I didn't. Part of me wondered if I had imagined him saying that to me at the airport. The other part thought maybe it was just something people say. *See you later. Talk soon. Take care. I'll call you.* All the same shit.

My mind spun with scenarios of how our text battle would play out, until the jostling of the bus lulled me to sleep.

An aggressive shake rattles me from my slumber. "We're here," the bus driver says gruffly. *Shit.*

Wearily, I make my way off the bus with my duffle bag and hail a cab outside the station. I'm excited to see my mom, but also scared. I'm afraid of what she will look like after my three weeks away from her. What if she's deteriorated? What if she's frailer and more unstable than before? I'm hopeful this specialist in New York will renew our optimism – either with cutting-edge treatments or perhaps advanced chemo-therapy trials that aren't as corrosive. This is not the first time my mom has battled this disease, and I remember last time how paper-thin her skin became, so thin it was almost translucent, how she lost all her hair from chemo and could barely get out of bed for days, how she was too weak to walk down a flight of stairs so we turned our living room into a bedroom for her. Our home became a hospice and my dad and I were the caretakers. It was excruciating.

Ethan is also in the city, and although I wish I could say he's here for the same reason I am, I know he's really here to head to the Hamptons for the Fourth of July parties.

At least being here is better than flying back to LA. I am not ready to run into Asher and feel the surge of inevitable emotions bubble over. Even though I'm convinced he just wants to sleep with me, I still can't shake my absurd daydream that he's madly in love with me. But the words "college-aged boys" and "committed and stable" do not exist in the same sentence. *I should know better, yet I can't stop myself.*

If I continue down this path, I'm going to eventually convince myself these fantasies are *real* and I'm terrified of seeing Asher again and having rejection thrown in my face when they are not. How naïve I've been to think someone like Asher Aves wanted anything else from me other than sex. The signs were all there – sliding into my DMs, dropping bread-crumbs. *Fuckboy.*

Anger twists in my throat, and my breath labors when I replay his promiscuity in my mind. I have to stop myself because when I start thinking of him, I remember our last text exchange. I remember his jealousy and rage when he saw another boy's hands on me, and it makes me think he wants more than something casual. But even with that my doubt still wins: I don't think he wants to take this thing we started, this beginning of *us,* any further. And that possibility breaks me.

Male voices echo from the hallway, pulling me from my thoughts. Ethan is here, and judging by the sound of it, he's not alone. I roll my eyes at the thought of a bunch of dudes tumbling into our condo, boasting about how drunk they were the night before.

Here they come. In rolls Ethan, boisterous as ever, followed by a guy I don't recognize. Behind them walks Leo and Wyatt. And then, as if in slow motion, I watch Asher stride through the door.

What the actual fuck.

I'm peering up from my phone, watching the menagerie of twenty-something men parade by, not expecting to see the one person I was eager to avoid. As soon as he's through the door, his eyes meet mine like he's searching for someone. My stomach drops.

Oh, he knew I would be here, I seethe.

Confusion and anger roil through my head. Why did he not bother to tell me he would be here? Why did he want to hold the element of surprise against me?

He doesn't smile when he sees me. In fact, there's no change in expression whatsoever – just a cold, piercing glare.

I feel like an ant about to be zapped into oblivion by the concentrated sunbeam of a magnifying glass. I'm going to throw up or collapse, or both. If only there were a trap door under my feet that would allow me to disappear.

"Addison, are you headed out with Mom?" Ethan shouts from the living room. The boys are clustered around the television.

"Yeah, she's just finishing up a call," I say, trying to hold it together. I hope the quiver in my voice goes undetected. My mind wills me to leave the kitchen, but my feet are glued to the floor. I can feel him looking at me but I'm too paranoid to look up from my phone.

The door of the fridge opens, forcing me to tear my eyes from the screen.

"Hi," Asher says, his inflection so much heavier than a simple greeting.

"How are you?" he asks as if he didn't ream me out two nights ago over text.

"I'm great," I say. My tone is angrier than I intended. I

don't want to give him the satisfaction of knowing how much his callous rant hurt.

Asshole, I think, willing him to hear my thoughts.

I went back to my phone, hoping if I ignore him long enough, he'll get the hint and walk away. I'm minutes away from leaving with my mom for her doctor's appointment and I have zero desire to give him a second of my time or energy. I need to be strong. I can't let my emotions weaken me.

Asher leans against the counter, cracking open a drink, refusing to yield.

The awkward silence is killing me. *Fine.*

"I didn't realize you were in the city," I say, caving.

"I'm here with Ethan," he says, taking a sip.

Of course you are.

"We're driving out to the Hamptons tomorrow, and I had to ship my car back anyway."

I give him a judgmental look.

"Did you not have your G-Wagen on campus last semester?"

"I did."

"So, you shipped it back to LA for only a month?"

"What else would I drive?" he asks, like the idea of shipping his ride back and forth across the country only to drive it around for a few weeks was the obvious choice.

He is so, so cocky, and I'm growing bored of our pretend conversation.

"Have fun in the Hamptons," I say snidely and brush past him.

I peek my head into my parents' bedroom to see my mom still on the phone.

Dammit. Back to my room and back to my thoughts.

Years ago when my parents first bought this condo in New York, I secretly hoped it would eventually be mine.

"Can I have it one day?" I asked my mom, to which she laughed and said "doubtful." She loves New York City as much as I do. It's vibrant and gritty and electrifying and it makes me feel alive. Columbia should have been my top choice, not Harvard.

My parents told me they didn't care about our Harvard legacy – they had gone to Harvard, my brother went to Harvard – but I had a nagging feeling that if I didn't go too, they would be disappointed.

"I would kill to have been accepted to Harvard, Addison," Mira and Violet both said to me. I knew I was fortunate to have choices. But I wish I wouldn't have been accepted: then my choice would be easy. If I said yes to Columbia, my mom and I could live together in this condo, she would be close to this new cancer specialist, and I could keep tabs on her to make sure she's doing okay.

What if I go to Harvard and something happens to her while I'm away? What if she deteriorates again? What if no one tells me until it's too late?

If I could stay with her, I could take care of her. *She needs me.*

I can't help but feel I've made a huge mistake. The consistent knot of anxiety in my stomach, growing bigger by the day, doesn't help to convince me otherwise.

A soft, rasping knock sounds at my bedroom door, and I know it's not my mom. She's more of a *two knock warning before I swing open your door* kind of person.

"Come in," I say.

My door opens, revealing a pensive Asher leaning against the doorframe.

"Do you need something?" I ask with irritation as he steps into my room, then perches against the wall like he's studying me. The hair atop his head is longer than I remember it and I find myself yearning to run my fingers through the dark strands.

"What was that about?"

"What?" I feign.

"I was talking to you, and you just walked away."

"Did I?" The sarcasm drips from my tongue.

"Look, I'm sorry I didn't tell you I would be here."

That wasn't half of it.

"Why would you be sorry? You don't need to tell me your whereabouts. It's not like I care."

I catch a muscle feathering in his jaw.

"You, on the other hand," I continue, eying my reflection in the mirror as I reapply my lip gloss, "seem to care a whole lot about where I am and who I'm with."

I try not to look over as his piercing, hazel-green eyes glare at me, threatening to shatter my glass mirror.

"I'm sorry I didn't call you." His tone is cold and hushed.

"Why? I wasn't expecting you to," I reply, now spritzing on more perfume. "We don't need to pretend that night was anything more than what it was," I say in the most nonchalant tone I can muster.

"Is that how you think I feel?" he asks quietly. I can't tell if I'm successfully getting under his skin or if this is normal conversation for him.

"I don't presume to know how you feel about me, Asher," I snort, toeing a precarious line. I doubt I can keep my act going much longer.

"Addison, you ready?" my mom calls, rescuing me.

"Coming," I yell back.

"I have to go," I say curtly as I prepare to leave. He doesn't move, doesn't leave as I leave. His eyes only trail me like daggers as I march past. He's lingering in my room and I can feel the weight of him.

"Bye, Mom!" Ethan calls. "Addison, why are you so dressed up?"

"I'm not dressed up, Ethan, this is just how I look."

"Okay," he says in that mocking voice of his.

We rush out the door, but not before I see Asher striding down the hallway. His menacing swagger tells me our rendezvous this weekend is far from over.

CHAPTER 12

Asher

I DESERVED THAT. I more than deserved that. But I'm not letting her get away so easily.

Yes, my timing today was unfortunate. I probably should have called her, or at least texted. But after the little stunt she pulled a few nights ago, I was worried my temper would get the best of me if I didn't let myself cool off.

What the fuck is a guy who looks like a goddamned male doll doing at nerd camp?

She knew what she was doing with those social media posts. I made the mistake of screenshotting them because I knew they would expire in twenty-four hours. When I looked at them again this morning, it took every ounce of willpower not to find this guy and threaten to bury him and his entire family. If I see evidence of him getting too close to her again, I may not be so restrained next time.

I walk back into the living room and Ethan's giving me a look like he knows whose room I was just in. He hasn't said anything to me since his last rant three weeks ago, but then again, I haven't done anything new to warrant a fresh tongue lashing. I'm sure he'll sniff me out soon enough, perhaps literally as he did the last time I set foot in Addison's room back in LA.

In my head, I'm penciling out how I'm going to ditch Ethan and this motley crew when my phone buzzes.

Please do not take any more of my underwear. I'm running painstakingly low as it is.

My lips twitch upward at her text.

You did leave your room unguarded, I text back.

I'm serious, you kleptomaniac.

Well, I guess you did say please.

I hate you.

Ouch, princess. Tell you what, you let me pick you up later tonight for a drive and I won't pilfer any more of your precious panties.

The three dots are killing me. I can tell she's debating my proposal.

Fine. What time?

Victory is mine, and I smile.

What time does your mom go to sleep?

10.

Then, 10:30?

She ends our text exchange with an eye roll emoji that has me grinning like a schoolboy.

"What the fuck are you smiling about?" Ethan barks. I look up, unaware he'd been watching.

"Don't worry about it," I say, putting my phone back in my pocket. The look he gives me could kill a bear in its tracks.

———

I'm waiting for her in my G-Wagen outside her parents' condo. Ditching Ethan and the gang wasn't easy. I made up an excuse I was meeting a girl I started seeing recently. *Not entirely a lie.* Ethan practically snarled at me, and I'm starting to think he's going to be a bigger problem than I anticipated.

I see her exit through the revolving doors of the building clad in those short jean shorts she likes to wear and a loose, white button-down.

"Hi," she says, climbing in. My car is suddenly flushed with an intoxicating scent of juicy, vanilla roses.

"You smell good," I say, giving her a warm smile. I notice the edges of a lacy bra peeking out of her button down and I find myself regretting the deal I made earlier.

"Where are we going?" she asks.

"Around," I smirk. I don't actually have a plan other than to keep her next to me for as long as possible.

Too many minutes pass by in silence.

"So, who's the guy?" Of all the paths I could've chosen to start our conversation, this was probably not the best. She gives me a scathing look.

"The guy you *screamed* at me about over text?"

"The one who looks like the prodigy of a male doll and a squirrel? Yes."

"He does not look like that *at all*."

"Are you going to answer my question?"

"I don't owe you an answer."

"Careful," I say, clicking my tongue.

"Why do you care who he is?"

"Because he was practically groping your ass in every picture you posted," I say, feeling my temper flutter.

"And?" she sneers.

"So you admit it?"

"Admit what? That I went out dancing with my friends and one of them happens to be attractive?"

"Ah, so you *do* think he's attractive?"

Oh, I'm definitely tracking this kid down now.

"Is there something going on between you two I should know about?"

"Why do you think you're entitled to know anything

about me, let alone my relationships with other guys?" she barks and I love how easy it is to get a rise out of her.

"You're in a RELATIONSHIP?"

"What? No. But do I find him cute? Absolutely."

My grip tightens on the steering wheel and if it weren't nighttime, I'd probably see my knuckles had gone white.

"I really don't know what your problem is, Asher."

I roll my neck at the sound of my name on her lips.

"It was one night. One. Night," she says, as if our night together meant so little to her.

"It wasn't one night to me, Addison," I say, glancing over. Her eyes glitter with every passing streetlight as she takes in the scenes of Manhattan nightlife: lively restaurants spilling out onto the sidewalk, passersby standing in groups, bouncers waiting outside bars.

"You confuse me, Asher," she says softly.

I find a relatively quiet block and pull over.

"I'm sorry I didn't call you," I say, taking her hand in mine and kissing it like I had when I drove her to the airport.

"I was stupid to think you would."

I wince at her response. I don't know why I didn't call her. I meant to, but days turned into weeks. When I didn't hear from her either, I convinced myself she wasn't interested. And why would she be? Addison can have any guy she wants so why would it be me?

It's probably for the best. Knowing my luck, everyone I've ever given a shit about has left. My biological dad left me when I was three. After seven years of scraping by, my mom moved the two of us to LA, claiming she met someone online. A year later, she married my stepdad, Steve, and never looked back. I didn't fault her for it and wanted her to be happy. I just didn't realize happy meant leaving for weeks or even months at a time to stay on set with Steve wherever his latest movie production was filming. I hadn't expected her vision of a new happy life in LA, a new beginning for her, to not include me.

They all leave in the end, so why would I expect my luck with Addison to be any different?

So, I didn't call her, didn't text, until my jealousy got the best of me.

"Is that how you truly feel, Addison? That it was just one night?"

She turns toward me, and I hold my breath, wondering if she knows how badly I need to hear it was more than a one-night fling for her.

"I don't know what's going on with us. I hardly know you."

I smile at her use of the word *us.*

"What is it you want to know? I'm an open book."

"Something tells me you are the opposite of an open book," she says, rolling her eyes. "I heard my brother tell my mom today he's thinking of staying in New York City for the rest of the summer because you and a bunch of other friends from Harvard will be here."

"And?"

"So you won't be in LA?" There's trepidation in her voice.

"I'm sure I'll come out for a weekend or two but I'm here to work on my startup."

"You have a startup?"

"It's fledgling at best."

"What is the business?"

"It's complicated."

"Oh no! My little girl brain can't possibly understand big, complicated things," she says with enough sarcasm to sink a ship.

"Sorry, I forgot who I was talking to," I grin. Addison's intelligence is well known. I'm three years older than her, yet she was in all my AP science classes in high school. Granted, sciences aren't entirely my forte, but I can run circles around computer programmers three times my age. Faced with endless hours of alone time growing up, I taught myself how to code, and programming soon became a second language. Once that started to feel mundane, I started hacking. It's comical how easy it is to hack into just about every public and private system out there. Then that became boring, so I started day trading. When I played the abandonment card, guilting my mom into giving me more of my stepdad's money to use as practice was not hard.

It was only a matter of time before I put the pieces together. The first iteration of my technology was computer software that automated my day trades based on stock price movements. I kept refining, and soon it could pinpoint micro-movements that went unnoticed by the big brokerage houses. That's when I began to notice correlations no one else seemed to see – infinitesimal links between stock prices and terrorism events.

"It's a terrorism monitoring technology that tracks micro-movements in the stock market in order to pinpoint terrorism strikes before they happen."

"Wow," she says, taken aback. "I would not have expected that."

"Does it surprise you coming from someone like me?"

"What does that mean? Someone like you?"

"I don't know, people tend to think I'm a dumb jock."

"Why? Because you're hot and ripped?" she blurts out.

"You think I'm hot and ripped?" I give her a knowing smile.

"Please. Me and the rest of the world. Like you don't know. But seriously, this is fascinating. How far along are you with the technology?"

"Well, in truth I've been at it for a while now but I only realized the potential of turning it into a business within the last year or so. I spent most of my sophomore year busting my ass to work through the kinks. There is this incredible econ professor at Harvard who's one of my mentors. He helped me get into Oxford."

"Oxford?" she asks.

"I'm doing my spring semester abroad there to work under this acclaimed professor. He has a known track record for getting financial technology startups like mine into YC."

"What's YC?"

"Y-Combinator. It's the most prestigious startup accelerator out there. I'm trying to get accepted to their program next summer so I can start fundraising."

"Holy shit," she exclaims. "I'm impressed."

A wholesome smile spreads across my face, and I think this is what pride feels like. I've never felt that before. In fact, the only real motivator has been throwing my success back in my biological father's face. *Vengeance can be a fucked-up cheerleader.*

"That says a lot coming from the woman who's going to cure cancer."

She scoffs. "I can only dream."

The mood shifts, and I feel a heaviness between us.

"How did your mom's appointment go today?" I ask.

"Good," is all she offers but the look on her face is a tangle of emotions.

"What's this?" I ask, skimming the lacy top of her bra with my forefinger. I've barely been able to take my eyes off it since she got in the car.

She looks down but doesn't answer.

"Unbutton your shirt," I gently command, pulling her button down open. The loose collar of the shirt dips down her shoulder, exposing her skin to the orange glow of the street-lamp above. Her collar bone accentuates every rise and fall of her chest and for a moment, time stops. Nothing could be more beautiful than watching the faint movement of her supple breasts as she breathes.

I trail my forefinger on top of her bra and ever so gently pull it down, exposing her breast. The buttery lace manages to feel rough against the velvety smooth skin surrounding her nipple, now agonizingly hard as I trace my thumb over it.

I swallow, my throat excruciatingly dry as I take in the perfect teardrop shape of her breast.

"Kiss me," I manage, my voice cracking like it did when I was fourteen.

Her hands wrap around my neck, pulling me across the center console as our mouths crash together. *Hungry.* We were both so hungry for each other. The soft moan she releases when my tongue tastes hers sends a lance of fire down my groin, and the press of my dick against my shorts aches.

My hand fondling her breast becomes greedy and starts savagely shoving into the top of her shorts when she pushes me away.

"It's late. I should get home," she pants.

I slowly recoil into the driver's seat and clamp my eyes shut until my heartrate is steady enough to drive.

"Give it to me," I say gruffly as I tilt my head in her direction.

"Give what to you?"

"Your bra."

"We had a deal!" she protests.

Fine, we did have a deal. I'll have to use another one of her undergarments I already have when I stroke my cock later.

I shift my car into drive, and we spend the rest of the ride back to her parents' condo in silence – me, tracing small circles across the back of her hand with my thumb, and her looking out the window. Both of us know whatever is happening between us just got considerably more complicated.

We pull up outside the condo building, and she hesitates.

"Try not to send me another bunch of rage texts," she says, unbuckling her seatbelt.

"Don't give me a reason to," I respond.

"You're incorrigible," she chides, stepping out of my car. She shuts the door and gives me a shy goodbye wave before disappearing into the building.

It's cute she thinks I'm joking.

I'm not.

CHAPTER 13

Addison

I MAKE the grave mistake of following him on social media. Down, down, down I went into the rabbit hole of past posts: the girls on his lap, the frat parties, the questionable substances. Is this who he truly is behind the mask he wears around me? The Asher who told me he wished I was his first, last, and only meal for all eternity?

Is this the Asher who cradles my hand and looks at me with a desperately sad longing I've never seen before?

I suppress the urge to vomit. This image of him, this partying frat boy surrounded by other women, makes me physically ill. I am not the sorority girl, the groupie, or the popular, social butterfly with men wrapped around her finger. I've never been the type to ooze confidence and the promise of a good time – not even before the incident.

I'm the girl who throws up a middle finger when men tell me to "smile more." I'm told the cold disdain I wear across my face on a daily basis could gut someone like a fish. My tolerance for dumb and arrogant rivals my social life – nonexistent.

Despite all this, I've somehow managed to fall for the fuckboy frat king. I've been drinking in his lies like a dog lapping up water on a hot day, in spite of my internal voice screaming at me to run.

After seeing him last week, then bearing witness to the debauchery of his Hamptons trip via social media, I'm seriously questioning my intelligence.

Girls pouring alcohol down his throat. Girls atop his shoulders at a pool party while playing a game of chicken. Half-naked, maybe completely naked, it was impossible to tell.

But what kills me is the fact that he knows I can see everything he's doing. And he *still* posts anyway.

The fact that he had the *gall* to rage text me over a few of my posts – which didn't even hold a candle to his level of scandal – is infuriating.

I want to unfollow him. But then he'll know I care. The problem is, I do. I care way more than I should, and I feel powerless against my emotions. Each new post is a dagger in my heart, twisting and twisting and twisting.

I hate him. *I. Hate. Him.*

————

"Let's go to that warehouse club again," I suggest to Ava at lunch.

The sexual tension between Gavin and I has all but burnt out, and I can tell he's intentionally avoiding me. I honestly didn't think one harmless kiss would cause such awkwardness. He's good-looking but not *that* good-looking.

I mean, fine, he's really good-looking. But what does that make me?

"Ava, am I ugly?" I blurt out.

"What?!" she laughs, caught off guard. "No! Are you insane? You look like a model, Addison. I would kill to have a drop of your beauty."

I blush, worried Ava will think I'm fishing for compliments. I know I sound obnoxious but I can't stop myself.

"Gavin must think I'm ugly. He's clearly avoiding me."

"Boys are stupid, Addison. STUPID. Don't give a six the satisfaction of thinking he can pull tens."

"What?" I look at her in confusion.

"Gavin is a solid six. He's cute in a boyish sort of way. Very confident in himself obviously. But you're a ten, Addison. And not an Ohio ten. You're a New York ten. He'll probably never do better. When he's stuck with a San Francisco seven, he's going to look back on this summer and curse himself for rebuffing you like he has."

"Thanks, Ava," I sigh, giving her a small smile. I have no clue what her number system means when it comes to ranking attractiveness but it sounds flattering.

"And yes, we should go back to the warehouse club. It's the last weekend of the program!"

Seconds later, she looks down at her phone.

"Malik's in. I just texted him. Oh, he says Gavin wants to come as well."

Great.

"Should I tell him Gavin's not invited?" she asks.

"It's fine," I bemoan.

"It'll be fun," Ava adds with a wicked smile, not bothering to look up from what I assume is a titillating text exchange with Malik. I love that the two of them think they are being so discrete. In reality, they're the most obvious secret love affair on the planet.

———

"WHAT?" I scream into the phone, huddled in the quietest nook I can find within the giant warehouse.

The line goes silent, and I'm assuming he hung up.

"What's going on?" Ava yells over the music when I turn around.

I shrug my shoulders and give a dismissive wave. She

tugs me back on the dance floor where an inebriated Gavin and Malik wait. We're all drunk at this point. My phone tells me it's 2:06 am when I feel it vibrate again in my belt bag.

He's called at least ten times in the last ten minutes, and I feel a vengeful smile spread across my face.

To say Gavin has been flirting with me tonight is an understatement. He can't keep his hands off me, and I'm happy to let him if it means I can document his lust for a certain someone to see on social media.

Payback is a bitch.

It's after three in the morning by the time we leave and pile into a rideshare vehicle.

"Guys, we will be home in like five minutes," I hiss. I couldn't care less if Ava and Malik are making out beside me, but their groping has dramatically escalated in the last thirty seconds.

Ava pulls away, giggling like a schoolgirl.

"SoOOO sorry to ooooffennnndd your pruUdishhh sensi-bilitieeees," she slurs.

I'm not a prude. I just don't want to be sitting beside you as Malik shoves his hand down your pants.

Gavin turns around, smirking at me.

This ride cannot be over fast enough.

"Finally!" I exclaim as I throw open the car door and jump out.

Malik and Ava waste no time. They nearly send each other tumbling to the ground as they sprint inside.

"They really hit it off this summer," Gavin says.

"I'd say."

I reach for the dorm door, but I'm tugged backward. Suddenly Gavin's arms are around my waist, and he's looking at me like he's about to kiss me.

"I should get to bed," I say, trying not very hard to pull away.

"I think you should come back to my room," he smiles.

An unmistakable feeling settles in my gut – a feeling I know should not be there. *Guilt.* Why does the thought of going back to Gavin's room make me feel *guilty?* Why does the thought of kissing him feel wrong?

Worst of all, why do I no longer *want* to kiss him? Three Saturdays ago, I was ready to kiss him and then some. But the idea of kissing someone other than Asher feels icky. It's not betrayal I feel, but sadness. It's a longing for the butterflies crashing around in my stomach at his touch. I want that heat pulsing under my skin when his lips part mine. It's a craving for that blood-boiling desire throbbing at my core, begging for him to explore my body, to take, to taste, to push inside me until I burst.

It's him. It's only him who can save me and I'm *dying.*

God, I hate that I feel this way, but I do.

"I can't, Gavin, I'm sorry."

He looks at me with the expression of someone who has never been rejected before.

"Seriously?" he scoffs.

I furrow my brows, confused.

"Um, yes."

"Whatever, Addison. I was only trying to be nice because I felt bad for you a few weeks ago when you tried to kiss me. I was never into you anyway."

I practically fall on my ass in disbelief.

He flings open the door to go inside.

A pity hookup? I was a pity hook-up? The absolute audacity.

I'm in such shock, I choke on a bug because I've been staring into space with my mouth gaping open.

"Shit, my phone's ringing again," I mutter. *Asher. I forgot he called me twenty times tonight like a fucking psycho.*

"You really are a fickle bitch, aren't you, universe?" I gripe toward the sky with my arms outstretched in surrender.

Against my better judgment, I answer.

"What do you want, psycho?"

He's quiet for a second before launching into a sinister laugh. It's the kind of laugh I would expect a serial killer to make when you try to fight back.

"What the fuck was that tonight, Addison?"

"What was what?"

I'm glad I'm drunk for this conversation because I have every intent of calling him out on his bullshit.

"Are you with him right now?"

"With who?"

Oh, this is going to be fun.

"Answer the FUCKING QUESTION. ARE YOU WITH HIM RIGHT NOW?"

I want to laugh because I've never heard him shout like this at anyone, let alone me. I can't tell if I'm amused or scared.

"Are you okay?" I choke out in a laugh.

"Where are you right now?" he demands. I can feel his rage seep through the phone.

"I'm not telling you where I am."

"Never mind, I know where you are. I'll be there in three and a half hours, and you better pray I don't find you with that fucking blonde doll of yours."

"Or what?"

"Are you fucking serious? Does he have a death wish, Addison?"

"Wait, how do you know where I am?"

"I built a fucking surveillance technology company, Addison, I know where everyone is."

"I can't tell if you're joking or…"

Through the phone, I hear the roar of a car ignition, followed by screeching tires. Suddenly I'm feeling very, very sober.

"Whoa, whoa, whoa. STOP DRIVING! ASHER, STOP DRIVING!" I could be wrong, but my guess is he is in no condition to drive.

More car noises.

"I'm not with him!" I shout. The thought of him driving like this launches me into a panic as images of Asher in the driver's seat of his hunter green G-Wagen, bloody and dead, flash across my mind.

"I'm not with him!" I plead, screaming into the empty night. "Pull over, please, Asher. I'm begging you. Pull over." My voice is ragged.

"I warned you what would happen," he snarls.

I feel a small wave of relief when the background noise quiets.

"That's not fair, Asher," I wail into the phone, my earlier resolve now completely shattered. "Your social media is swarming with women. It's practically all you post!"

"It's different, Addison," he sneers. "I don't know those girls. They mean nothing to me. I have zero interest in them. *You* told me *you* were attracted to this guy. Do you remember what you said when I asked if you've fucked him?"

I did.

"Not yet," Asher answers for me. "You said *not yet.* I'm not FUCKING any of these girls, Addison, nor do I want to."

"Liar," I cut in.

"Liar?" he asks as if it's the most preposterous thing he's ever heard. "I've been called many things, but liar is not one of them."

I doubt that.

"So I'm going to ask you one last time. Where. Are. You?"

I sigh, exasperated. "I'm standing outside the dorm. By myself."

"It's four a.m.," he says coldly.

"It's four a.m.!" he shouts as if I didn't hear the first time. "And you're standing outside, in the dark, alone? Bullshit."

"It's not bullshit. We just got home, and I saw you calling so I answered. Everyone else went inside."

"Is he waiting for you?"

"No, I assume he went to bed."

"And is he waiting for you to join him there?"

"No!" I say loudly. Boy, did I lose this fight. "No," I say again in surrender.

"Please don't drive down here," I beg. He has yet to convince me he won't. "Drive down tomorrow if you want but not tonight. I can't imagine you're in any condition to drive."

"Go up to your room, get in bed and call me. *With video*," he adds. "If I don't hear from you in fifteen minutes, your little friend is a dead man."

CHAPTER 14

Asher

LIKE A GOOD GIRL, she did as she was told.

I haven't decided what I'm going to do to the guy yet as punishment for thinking he could have her. But I do know a lot of people at Stanford who owe me favors.

"Satisfied?" she huffed when she called me back.

"Hardly," I told her.

I was *hardly* satisfied and I wouldn't be satisfied until she was mine.

"I'm sorry about the videos I posted tonight," she says remorsefully.

"It's not the documentation I'm upset about. It's the fact it was happening at all. You were so obviously flirting with him. Are you interested in him?"

"No."

"Then why?"

"I don't know."

"To get back at me for some dumb social posts on my grid with a bunch of strangers?"

"I'm sorry," she said again. That's twice now.

"Don't apologize to me. Apologize to your friend when I break his fucking legs."

"Don't break his legs," she whispers. I try to reel my temper back, worried I've pushed her too hard. She's exhausted, and I can tell she's about to fall asleep by how heavy her eyelids look.

"I'll settle for a few fingers."

"You're ridiculous."

Once again, she thinks I'm joking.

"Are you flying back to LA at the end of this or coming to New York?"

"LA."

"I'll have to fly out there, then."

She's nearly asleep.

"Princess," I say loudly into the phone. Her eyes flutter awake. "Go to bed, I'll text you this week to make plans."

"Okay," she hides a yawn with her hand. "Goodnight, Asher."

"Goodnight, beautiful," I say as she ends the call.

———

My phone rings, and I wake up to see my mom calling. She rarely does, so this is concerning.

"Mom," I say gruffly into the phone.

"Long night, Asher?" she asks.

"You could say that," I say, rubbing the sleep from my eyes. I have no idea what time it is. The last I remember, I was looking at flights to LA.

"I have something I need to tell you."

The reservation in her voice makes me worried.

"Your dad died."

"Steve?" I throw the covers off. "What happened?"

"Not Steve. Steve is fine. Your biological father. He passed away on Friday, and I got the news yesterday."

"Oh, thank god," I say, clutching my chest. "Mom, don't scare me like that, Jesus Christ."

"Are you... upset?" she asks tentatively.

"About my sperm donor? How could I be upset when I barely knew the guy?"

"Well, I know you had...," she pauses. "Perhaps some pent-up resentment toward him for what he did. Some unresolved... frustration."

I can tell she's being careful with her words. The therapist she forced me to see when I was a boy, claiming I had *anger issues* due to my piece of shit sperm donor, is still a source of strife between us.

"Honestly, Mom, I don't give two shits about him. One less deadbeat dad in this world, the better."

Except the deadbeat part only pertained to me. Ten years after he left, I found out he remarried, moved to St. Louis, shacked up with some suburban trophy wife who left her husband for him, and they went on to have four kids together. Four half-siblings. I have four half-siblings whom I've never met. They have zero idea I even exist.

"Okay, well, I'm sorry to tell you this over the phone. How is everything in New York?"

"Great, Mom," I answer, flopping back down on my bed.

"All right, I can tell you want to go. Asher?"

"Yes?"

"Slow down on the partying, won't you? It makes me worried."

"Mom, I'm not partying. *That much*," I add for the sole purpose of getting under her skin.

"Asher, I'm serious. I don't want to find you dead in a ditch somewhere."

"Wow, Mom. Morbid. This conversation has taken a turn for the worse so I'm going back to bed."

"It's eleven a.m. there."

Is it? Shit.

"Goodbye, Mom," I say and hang up.

Well. This is quite the plot twist.

It shouldn't upset me, yet the news consumes me from the inside out. Every early morning, every late night, every second of pushing myself harder and farther than I thought possible was so that one day I could savor the sweet taste of revenge. The fire fueling my drive, to become someone so successful it would bring him to his knees with remorse, just went out.

Typical.

It's just like him to leave before the fucking party even starts.

CHAPTER 15
Addison

I'M NOT sure if Asher is of sound mind. I don't know what happened over the last two weeks but I'm pretty sure he's found his rock bottom.

He keeps posting videos to his socials of him and his friends partying to the point of unconsciousness and I'm starting to think he's the one with a death wish. After another stretch of radio silence, I mustered the courage last night to text him and ask why he had a busted lip. In his latest video, he looks like he's been cage fighting.

I found your Stanford friend and made good on my promise, was his only response.

I didn't have it in me to banter back. He didn't seem to care whether I texted him, or even existed for that matter.

He didn't seem to care at all.

I vomited again this morning from another nightmare.

This time, Connor's knife was pressed against my throat, the cold steel digging into my skin with each swallow. A warm trickle crawls down my neck, and my vision blurs in and out as my eyes fall to his hand holding the blade. My hands shake uncontrollably, my knees threatening to buckle. I can't black out. If I collapse, I don't know what he'll do to me. *He'll…*

Black.

Dread. Horror.

I'm screaming, but I'm stuck inside my body, paralyzed.

He lifts the knife above my chest.

Awake.

Sweat coats my skin, my pillow, my sheets. My T-shirt is drenched, clinging to my body.

I barely make it to the toilet in time.

It's August now, and I leave for Harvard in one week. *One week.* Incoming students have to be there early for orientation.

Harvard, where I'll be alone and three-thousand miles away from my mom, is a mistake.

A horrible, terrible mistake.

———

Dr. Mindy's office smells of recently burned palo santo like it usually does.

"Addison, nice to see you," Dr. Mindy says as she comes to fetch me from the waiting room. "It's been a while since we've seen each other."

I sink down into a well-worn cushion on the familiar brown leather couch.

"I know," I admit. I haven't talked to Dr. Mindy since the beginning of summer, before Johns Hopkins.

"So how have you been?" she asks.

I let out an extended breath. "I think I made a mistake with Harvard."

"Why do you think that?" she probes gently.

"I don't think I can be so far away from my mom. I'm worried something is going to happen to her while I'm away and I won't be able to get home in time."

"Has her condition worsened?"

"No. It's been relatively the same for the past six or eight months. We saw a new cancer specialist a few weeks ago in New York actually. It was promising. There might be a new treatment she can try."

"That sounds positive."

A silence passes between us.

"Is there more you're not saying?"

I close my eyes and take in another long inhale. "The nightmares are back."

"Oh," she says. "And how long have they been going on this time?"

I shrug. "I don't know, six months, maybe more."

I look out the row of floor-to-ceiling windows at the massive church across the street. The towering stone temple is perched at the top of a grass-covered slope. The sundrenched, green grass contrasts with the looming beige structure on Santa Monica Boulevard, and the whole image is permanently etched into my brain. The grass, the slope, the outline of the stone towers – reminders of a world passing me by while I struggle to get rid of the phantom hand clawing at my windpipe, waiting to crush me.

"I just thought they would be over by now," I say, my voice barely louder than a whisper.

My quivering lower lip threatens to undo me.

"I can't do this. I can't go."

Dr. Mindy hands me a box of tissues.

"Is going to a different school still an option?"

"No, not now. I think I need to complete one year before applying for transfers."

"Can you defer? Take a gap year?"

"Maybe."

I grab another handful of tissues. The wad I'm clutching is on the verge of disintegrating.

"Why don't you look into that option? Another year at

home could be good for you, and you'll be able to see your mom every day."

I nod.

"Tell me about the nightmares," she says. "Are they the same as before?"

I nod again, clearing my throat. "Yes. Sometimes I get away and I make it to the running part. Sometimes I become paralyzed, and he gets me. Or right before he gets me, I black out and I know... I know what he's going to do. And then I wake up."

"But he doesn't, or I should say, he *didn't* get you. In real life," Dr. Mindy says.

"Right?" she looks at me with emphasis. "He didn't get you in real life. You fought him. You got away."

"Right?" she repeats when I don't respond.

"But what if these dreams are a premonition? He's still out there," I weep.

I'm not crazy. I know he's coming back for me, to finish me. I can feel it.

"Repeat after me Addison: I got away. I fought back. I survived."

She doesn't understand.

I hate these words but I say them to make the exercise stop.

"I got away. I fought back. I survived," I say meekly.

"Again."

I repeat myself once, twice, three times before Dr. Mindy is satisfied.

It's a lie.

The version of myself I was before the incident did not survive.

Connor took her from me. Try as I might to convince myself otherwise, she did not make it out.

CHAPTER 16

Addison

WHEN DO *you get to Boston?* I read on my phone screen.

I've been staring up at the ceiling of my room for an hour now. Funny how things like the strange brown spots, unexplainable scuff mark, and remnants of glow-in-the-dark stars from ten years ago start to feel comforting when you've spent countless hours in this very same position, talking yourself off a ledge. I exhale a long, audible breath. *Familiar.*

I've Xanaxed myself into oblivion, and my anxiety has finally come down from my therapy session with Dr. Mindy when my phone dings.

Oh.

Him.

I'm not, I text back before thinking things through.

What do you mean you're not?

I'm not going.

To orientation?

To all of it. Harvard, orientation. I'm not going.

Maybe it's my imagination, but the three dots feel more frantic than usual. Then my phone is ringing.

I'm not ready for this. I'm not ready to face him.

I remind myself Asher doesn't care about me, so why should I care about telling him?

I take a breath and will myself to answer.

"He does exist."

That's the Xanax talking.

"What's going on? Did something happen with your mom?"

"No, she's fine. I mean, she's not fine but she's not worse."

"So I'll ask you again then. What's going on?"

"Nothing. Everything. Life."

"Stop fucking with me, Addison. Are you serious?"

"About what?"

"Jesus Christ. About not coming to Harvard."

"Oh, that. Very serious."

"Why?"

"Because."

"ADDISON, what is *wrong* with you? Are you okay? Why do you sound so groggy? Have you been drinking?"

"Drinking? No, that's you, Asher."

"Funny."

"Is it?"

"I swear to god, Addison," I hear him mumble.

"I'm fine. It's the anxiety medication."

"Are you seriously not coming, Addison?"

"My mom's not well, and I don't want to be so far away from her."

"Bullshit."

"*What?* How dare you? What is wrong with you?"

"What are you going to do if you don't go to Harvard?"

"I don't know. I haven't gotten that far. Take a gap year. Reapply to Stanford."

"The fuck you will. Addison, do not think for a second I won't fly out there and drag your ass to Boston."

I laugh at how outlandish he sounds. "Asher, if you can't

pick up your phone and text me then you're sure as shit not flying out here and dragging my ass *anywhere*."

"Mmmhmm, keep talking, princess."

"You're such a joke, Asher."

"Is that so? Well, I hope you're prepared to laugh your ass off because this joke just booked a plane ticket. I'll be there by morning, Addison, so pack your *fucking bags*."

––––––

Why am I smiling?

I curse my Xanax for robbing me of the panic attack I should be having right now.

He's not actually coming here, Addison, the small voice in the back of my head says, tethering me back to reality. It was your imagination.

This time, I agree with the small voice, feeling my eyelids grow weary and my head grow heavy against the silky soft pillowcase.

––––––

Open your fucking door or I'm ringing the doorbell.

I read this text message as I hear my mom speaking to someone in that formal voice she uses with everyone outside our immediate family.

The familiar thump of feet up the stairs sends my eyes wide.

"Come in," I say to the loud two knocks at my door. I know she's going to barge in anyway.

Her heather blue bathrobe is cinched tight around her waist, and she carries the scent of freshly brewed coffee when she opens my bedroom door.

"Addison," her voice is hushed but hurried as she slips

into my room and gently closes the door behind her. "You have a visitor."

I'm looking at her like I've seen a ghost.

"Who?" I mouth. She shoots me a look like I obviously know who it is and have a boatload of explaining to do.

"Do you want to tell me why Asher Aves is at our house at seven in the morning asking to see you?"

She's not buying my dumbfounded look.

"He said you were expecting him?"

"Shit," I say, throwing off the covers. "Tell him I'll be down in ten minutes."

I race to the bathroom. "Mom," I hiss under my breath. "Do NOT tell Ethan."

She rolls her eyes at me and makes her way back downstairs.

Shit.

Shit. Shit. Shit.

————

"Oh, Addison, there you are," my mom says a little too eagerly.

I pad into the kitchen, and the absolute shock written all over my face earns me a cocky, ear-to-ear grin.

"Asher says you promised him a beach day before leaving for Harvard?"

I did?

I glance at Asher, confused.

"That she did," he says with a heart-melting grin, which I'm sure is for my mom's benefit. "I told her how much I missed the beach, especially during Boston winters."

Oh, this is so awkward. And he's just sitting there, smug as a cat who just backed his mouse into a corner.

"Well, how lovely," my mom says, standing. "Addison," she continues, "you know your dad and I have the event downtown this evening, right? We have to leave around four so we may not see you when you return from the beach. Or, whenever you return," she smirks, and I watch her saunter away. I feel my entire body flush with embarrassment. *I am mortified.*

My gaze snaps back to the grinning cat now sucking every last drop of oxygen from the room. I've yet to move any closer. As I watch him stand, my heart pounds, beating so hard against my ribcage it might actually tear a hole through my chest. *Is this what a heart attack feels like?*

I swallow, my head titling back as he nears. Nothing makes sense. Why is he *here?*

Oh god, and I smell him – the tobacco leather musk he wears.

This is not real. I am DREAMING.

I'm never taking Xanax again.

Mere inches separate our bodies. His fingertips touch the soft spot on my neck right below my earlobe, and I shiver as he drags them down my jawline, tilting my chin upward until our eyes lock.

"If I were you, princess," he whispers in my ear, his voice practically a growl. "I would be more careful the next time you decide to call my bluff."

CHAPTER 17

Addison

"WHOSE CAR IS THIS?" I shout over the roar of the wind whipping my hair around. The top of the convertible is down.

"Steve's," he shouts back.

"And he lets you drive it?"

"I'm driving it, aren't I?"

"Are we really going to the beach?"

"No, I fucking hate the beach."

Okay then.

He looks over at me as I wait patiently for an answer.

"I'm taking you back to my house. My mom and Steve aren't home, and I'd much rather swim in my pool than get sand all over my dick."

Fair enough. A sandy dick does sound… unpleasant.

I don't think my brother has ever been to Asher's house, which is strange given how close they seemed in high school.

Instead, I can only remember Asher sitting in our living room with Ethan and his friends, hollering at whatever sports game was on. As I'm replaying these memories, we pull into a driveway of what can only be described as a mansion.

"This is your house?!" I exclaim, shutting the car door.

"My prison, yes," he answers, not missing a beat. *Prison?* I tuck this comment away for examination at a later time. A keycode opens the front door, and I follow him inside in awe.

I speak before thinking. "How many people live here?"

"Just me," he smirks over his shoulder.

"*Just you?*"

"Well, it's Steve's house obviously but he's usually on set, and my mom likes to travel with him. Most of the time, it's just me."

"Did you throw huge parties here in high school?"

"Absolutely not. I don't want other people around my shit."

"Oh?" I raise a brow. "Is there a secret sex room here or something?"

"You wish," he chuckles.

"Kitchen is here, pool is that way, closest bathroom is down this hall. Make yourself comfortable. You want a water, coffee, beer?"

"Beer? It's not even nine a.m.!"

"I always forget you're such a rule follower."

"Are you going to show me your room?"

He leans against the kitchen counter, contemplating the question.

"Maybe."

"*Maybe?*"

"I told you I don't like other people around my shit."

"And you put me in the category of 'other people'?"

He must know I think this is odd behavior because he says, "I have a lot of personal stuff in there I've never shown anyone."

"Are you a serial killer?"

He throws his head back in laughter, and I find myself thinking it's the most genuine, beautiful laugh I've heard.

"Do you think you'd still be alive right now if I were?"

"I don't know," I shrug. "Maybe you like to play with your toys first."

"You have quite the disturbed mind, princess."

He ambles out of the kitchen, leaving me to contemplate my life choices.

"You coming, Carol Bundy?" he says. His voice sounds so loud in the empty space of the house it's alarming. If you lived here by yourself, what sound would fill the void? These rooms have no life to them, no warmth. This doesn't feel like a home. It's more like a... *prison*. The comparison clicks into place as we arrive at the end of a long corridor.

I watch him punch a set of numbers into a padlock and I don't know if I'm curious or terrified. Am I the dumbest person in history? This is literally the moment in every horror movie right before the girl gets an axe to the stomach.

The heavy door swings open, and I hesitate.

"Oh, for fuck's sake, Addison," he says, rolling his eyes. "It's just my room."

This isn't a room, it's a palace.

"Asher, this is as big as someone's apartment!"

"Mmm, it's a bit snug for my taste, but I've made it work."

I take in the massive, king-sized bed that anchors the middle of the room. The décor is surprisingly tasteful – minimalist but not sparse. A huge walk-in closet and lavish bathroom are nestled off to the side.

"Oh, wow."

Four computer monitors top an enormous wooden desk. Stacked on top of each other to make one large square, they display graphs and numbers that make me think of Wall Street.

Books and photos line the shelves nearby.

"Wow, your mom is really beautiful," I say, my eyes darting over old photos of Asher as a young boy with his mother. *Asher looks a lot like his mom.*

"People always tell me I look like her," he says. I look over to see Asher lying on his back atop his bed, gazing at the ceiling. *Familiar.*

"Who's that?" I ask, pointing to a framed picture of him and another boy in baseball uniforms posing for the camera. They're maybe seven or eight years old.

"That's my friend Joey. We went to school together in Chicago."

"Do you still keep in touch with him?"

"No, Joey was a pretty troubled kid. He was in juvie for a long time but I think he's in prison now."

"Oh," I say. A ripple of sorrow flickers across my chest.

An old Polaroid is tucked into the side of a picture frame at the back of a shelf, hidden from view by all the other photos of Asher and his mom. A man cradles a sleeping baby in his arms, staring down at the newborn with joy and wonder.

I part my lips in anticipation of the question about to tumble out of my mouth, but I stop myself. *This is not a happy memory.* I swallow, unable to shake the intrusive thought gnawing at me.

I notice there aren't any pictures of his LA friends. No Ethan, no Wyatt, no lacrosse team photos, no high school prom pictures. In fact, no recent pictures of him and his mom either.

The photos that are here aren't happy memories. They're *painful.*

I slowly turn around, wondering why he would intentionally choose to turn his room into a memorial of his abandonment, but Asher isn't looking at me.

I watch his torso rise and fall and wonder how he's able to fall asleep in this prison of his own making.

———

Time has managed to escape our grasp. I feel his body stir beside me, and it's enough to wake me up. A momentary panic sets in when I don't recognize my surroundings, but I feel the heat of his skin against mine and I remember.

His room. His bed.

He rolls onto his back, grunting at the realization we've slept half the day.

"Shit," he says, blinking awake. "I guess I was tired."

He groans into the crook of my neck as he pulls me against him, nuzzling my hair now tousled with sleep.

"Is this real or am I dreaming?"

"Is what real?" I ask.

"You," he says, breathing me in. "In bed with me."

It was such a simple question, but it felt so loaded.

"Mmm, I am so hungry. I'm ordering food for us." He scrolls through his phone, and suddenly I feel out of place. *What am I doing here?*

"Do you plan on taking me home today?" I ask.

"That depends," he says, still scrolling. "Do you plan on telling me what's going on with you today?"

Satisfied with whatever he ordered, he puts his phone back on the nightstand and turns toward me, propping his head on his elbow.

"And don't tell me it's your mom's health because we had quite the chat this morning waiting for your ass to get downstairs."

I look at him in anger. He has no right to talk to my mom about the state of her health.

"She was rather surprised to hear you were planning to take a gap year so abruptly, five days before the start of orientation."

I sit up, fuming. "You had no right to tell her. *I* haven't even told her!"

My mind is racing at the conversation I know I'm going to have when I get home.

"Calm down, baby," he says, placing his palm on the bend of my knee. "I didn't tell her."

"Why would you lie about something like that?"

"Why would you tell *me* you're not going to Harvard before you told your mom?"

He had a point. A dull ache thrums at my temples, and I feel backed into a corner.

"Addison, I cannot imagine how hard it is to watch your mother endure chemo and radiation and lord knows what other treatments. I'm not negating your worry and your fear of losing her. But whatever is going on with you is not just about her."

"She's doing okay right now," I admit.

I look at him, my knee curled to my chest, and feel my resolve slipping. His eyes say so much without uttering a word, and they strip me bare. His gaze wraps around me like a steel vine, unfurling the tension in my clenched jaw and rigid shoulders. *It's okay,* his expression says, *I've got you. You're safe with me.*

His hand slides down my thigh when I curl my other knee up to my chest. His touch, delicate and reassuring, is like a parachute. *Jump,* it says, *I will catch you.*

"My mom is part of the reason, but… there's more," I continue quietly. "I have very bad anxiety. I've had it for years after the thing happened with… you know, Connor." I hate saying his name aloud. And I hate what I'm about to say next but I can't stop myself.

I suck in a breath. "I'm worried…"

I try to suppress the lump in my throat, so I can squeeze out my next words. "I'm worried he'll find me again. And when he does…" my face crinkles as I take in a choppy inhale. "When he does, I don't know if I'll make it out next time."

My voice cracks with an overwhelming need to sob.

"I've tried to convince myself I got away that day because of all the Krav Maga training. He… he had a knife and he was going to make me," I swallow, shaking my head. It hurts too much to say what Connor was going to make me do. "But something happened. There was a noise in the hallway, and it was enough to make him stop for a second. Then before I could think, my knee just struck him between the legs, and maybe my self-defense skills helped somewhat. But deep down, I know the real reason I got away. It was luck. Pure. Luck."

I eke out a choked laugh at my honesty. I've never admitted this to anyone – not even Dr. Mindy. To others, I say I got away because I'm strong, a fighter, a survivor. I've shoved this lie down into the pit of my gut for the last three years and trapped it there, driving it further inside me and piling more pain on top of it. When it festers, I find other ways to torture myself until I've strangled the trauma into submission. But now, hearing myself say it out loud, it's as if something within me has splintered wide and is gurgling open, raw and agonizing. I don't know if it feels like relief or compunction.

Tears, hot and heavy, cradle my cheeks, and I remember I'm in Asher's bed, oversharing and unraveling into a mess.

I look at him again, figuring he'll pull away with awkward discomfort, but instead I see something unexpected. Not pity, not sorrow, not sympathy.

Ire.

CHAPTER 18

Asher

NEVER HAS my heart shattered so completely. Not when my dad left, not when my mom left, not when I begged god to take me from this earth because the thought of one more day alone in this *fucking house* was more torture than I could bear.

But I can't tell her. I can't tell her what I did to Connor. Not yet. Maybe not ever.

Seeing her like this, in so much pain, makes me want to do it again. It makes me want to *kill him*. That worthless bastard cannot be the reason she doesn't go to Harvard this year. Tears stream down her cheeks as she tells me her truth, and I rise to cup her face.

"Addison, look at me."

Her amber-brown eyes are filled with anguish as they meet mine and I know in this moment I will do anything, say anything, to take her pain away.

"I need you to know that piece of shit will never hurt you again. He'll never breathe the same air as you, be in the same place, or the same city, or even the same state as you. Not in this lifetime or the next, Addison. I promise you that. He will never come near you again."

"You don't know that, Asher," she whimpers.

"I'll be there with you Addison," I say. "I won't let anything happen to you." My eyes lock on hers so she knows I mean it.

She nods as I wipe her tears, but they don't stop.

"Addison," I exhale, resting my forehead against hers until the tips of our noses touch. "I need you to know you're safe. I will keep you safe. I promise."

Soft, delicate lips graze mine. I plant a gentle peck against her mouth in return, then another, then another, then another, until her lips part mine with silent confirmation.

I run my tongue over hers and fuse our mouths together, sealing in my promise, until our kisses turn hungry and her need is clear.

More.

More will take her pain away and I want to give her everything.

"Tell me how much of you I can take," I whisper into her ear. I cannot stop kissing her. I cannot stop breathing in her scent, the smell of her hair, the taste of her skin. My own need is crazed now, and if she doesn't tell me her boundaries up front, I won't be able to control myself.

I will take all of her.

She grabs the hair on the back of my head, pulling my mouth onto hers, and I can feel the entire girth of her tongue on mine. I kiss her hard for as long as I dare, then force myself to pull away.

"Tell me, Addison," I say, studying her face for any signs of hesitation. My chest is heaving but I swear I'm holding my breath.

She runs her hands down my neck without speaking until they rest on the front of my shoulders. Even through her T-shirt, I can see the tops of her breasts heaving. It feels as if my entire existence hinges on what she says next.

"Take everything."

CHAPTER 19

Addison

"TAKE EVERYTHING," I tell him.

Remnants of tears cling to my lashes, but his body – kissing me, pressing into me –feels so goddamn good. And *fuck*, why does he make me feel so safe?

He searches my eyes for hesitation I hope he doesn't find. I'm fully aware of the permission I've just granted, yet he still studies me.

"Do you know what *everything* means, Addison?" he asks.

I'm rather insulted by the insinuation until he says, "Because let me tell you what *everything* means to *me*."

He lowers his lips next to my ear, and I startle at the sensation of his fingertips grazing the fleshy part of my abdomen. He drags them upward lazily until they settle on my breast, easily tucking beneath the underwire of my bra to slide it over my nipple. His playful tugging elicits an instinctual arch of my back, and I am uncomfortably aware of the throbbing angst building between my legs.

He kisses that sensual spot of mine right behind my earlobe where my jaw meets my neck, and a small moan slips from my lips. Releasing me, he sits up. But the pause only lasts long enough for him to pull off my T-shirt and unhook my bra.

He nestles back against my side and gives my nipple a hard, merciless twist, drawing a whimper of want from my lips.

"Everything means these two fingers are going to explore each crease and crevice of your pussy until I'm convinced I've memorized every inch of you," he says, as the fingers responsible for the zinging pain in my now hard nipple trail their way down my stomach and begin tracing unhurried circles on the outside of my underwear. "I want to know exactly where to stroke you to coax out your orgasm."

A finger tucks beneath my underwear and barely parts me with infuriating restraint. Squeezing my eyes shut, I writhe around his fingertip, begging for more pressure. But he refuses.

"Then I want to know the precise location of the spot inside you that requires no coaxing whatsoever." I feel a bit more of him slide in and I groan with anguish.

"I want to know exactly how to rub your clit," his fingers mirroring his words, "to get you to finish as quickly or as slowly as I want. Because I plan on making you come whether we're fucking in bed with all the time in the world or on a thirty-second elevator ride."

"And once I'm satisfied I've found and committed all your pleasure points to memory and I've got you so wet it sounds like I'm dunking my hand into a bucket of water, then, Addison, I will take *all of you*."

"I'm going to fuck you in this bed until my sheets are soaked through and you're screaming my name so loud the neighbors down the hill can hear you. Once I let you finish, you're going to put on that little red bikini of yours and ride my dick around the pool like a jet ski. And last, but certainly not least, I'm going to throw you over my shoulder and carry you back inside to the kitchen and set you on the countertop, where I will proceed to untie every goddamn string of that red bikini with my teeth. And once I've admired you, dripping wet and naked, I'm going to pull up a stool and feast on you until I'm certain I've taken every last drop."

Yes, I think. *Yes, I want this. All of this.* I'm panting, desperate for the pressure he refuses to give me. I squeeze my fingernails into his forearm so hard I might draw blood.

"Is that what you want?" he asks.

"Yes," I say breathlessly, begging. His knowing grin has me undressed before his hands can reach my zipper, pulling off both my shorts and underwear at the same time.

I watch him stand, tugging off his own shirt and shorts as he takes out a condom from his bedside table. My shock at the sheer size of him is embarrassingly obvious, and I imagine I must look like one of those cartoons with eyes bulging out of their sockets.

He looks down at me and smirks and my face flushes with scalding heat. He repositions himself on top of me and lowers down until my breasts are pressed firmly against his pectorals. I feel his shaft rubbing against my groin and I'm already so wet, the slickness at my apex now coats my inner thighs.

"Then tell me what I want to hear, Addison."

"I want you," I breathe. "I want you so badly."

His mouth on top of mine curves into a wicked smile.

"I already know you want me. Try again."

I truly have no idea but I will say anything this man wants to hear.

"One week from now, where will you be?" he offers, giving me a hint.

He raises his hips to slide his hand between my legs, and I feel his fingers gently spread my labia apart.

I open my legs wider to angle my entrance upward, but again, he pulls back.

"Say it," he growls.

"Was it real? Your promise?" I ask in desperation. I don't want to give in, but he's pinned my hands together above my head and pinned my thighs apart with his knees. I know I'm helpless to do anything other than give him what he wants. But I need to hear him say that promise one more time. If he truly means it, then his feelings for me must be real. If going to Harvard gives me a chance to have more of him, I'll do it. I will go.

"Yes," he rasps. "I promise you, Addison, I will keep you safe. Now, *say it*."

"*Say. It,*" he snarls through clenched teeth as he teases me again with his fingertips. I release an exasperated groan.

"Harvard," I say, my voice breathy and hoarse.

"*Again.*"

"HARVARD," I say louder.

Another inch of his fingers, maybe two, pushes inside me, and I turn feral like a possessed woman during an exorcism.

"Now it's your turn to say you promise," he commands, squeezing my wrists harder as he slowly slides his fingers in and out.

Oh god, I can't take it. I'm already panting like a rabid dog.

"Please, Asher," I beg him. I want him. I need him. I'm going to lose my mind if I don't feel him push inside me in the next two seconds.

"*Say it, Addison.*"

"I promise! I promise, Asher! I'll go. I'LL GO. PLEASE JUST FUCK ME!"

He barrels his two fingers inside me all the way to the knuckles and I scream.

———

When I first envisioned what losing my virginity would be like, I doubt I dreamt of such vivid colors. My initial fantasy was likely painted on a two-dimensional canvas in shades of black, white, and gray. I am certain I did not imagine a three-dimensional sculpture glittering with every color of the rainbow like a unicorn in the sunshine.

I've explored myself before. But his two fingers swirled around a spot so sensitive it caused my entire abdomen to convulse and my nipples to harden into razor-sharp peaks. I moaned so loud I should have been mortified.

"There it is," he whispered into my mouth as I climaxed onto his fingers. My eyes were still shut as I heard the crinkle of a condom wrapper and felt the weight of his knees return to either side of my hips.

He had traversed my core with such voracity, I was already ripe and swollen with pleasure when I felt his length press against my opening and then begin to spread my walls apart.

"Fuck, Addison, you are so goddamn tight," he groaned as he carefully moved himself inward. I could feel his biceps quivering as he tried to restrain himself. It hadn't hurt yet, but I didn't realize my entire body had seized up. I was bracing in anticipation of the pain, when he paused inside me.

"Are you okay?" he had whispered.

I nodded.

"Does it hurt?"

"Not yet."

"Promise me you'll tell me to stop if it hurts."

I nodded again.

I felt him slide in further.

"Mmm," I winced.

"Addison?" he asked.

"I'm okay, I promise," I said. He looked at me like he didn't believe a word.

"There was a little discomfort just now but it doesn't *hurt* hurt."

His eyes were still fixated on mine, searching.

"Keep going," I had pleaded but it came out more like a whine.

Slowly. He went so slowly.

I find it hard to believe someone who looks like him could be so gentle and attuned to my needs and emotions. How can this be real? What did I do to deserve Asher Aves wanting to memorize every inch of my body for the sole purpose of mastering my pleasure, begging to caress my curves and taste my skin, telling me he plans drink my orgasms like lemonade on a hot day?

Yet here he was, spreading me like a book as he buried himself further and further inside me, creating room for himself until I no longer had any more room to give and he no longer needed it.

"You okay?" he whispered, his breath shaky.

"Yes," I answered back.

"You have all of me now," he said as he fluttered kisses among my lips, jawline, and neck. I wrapped my arms around him and pulled him close so I could bury my face into the curve of his neck.

"Fuck, Addison, I want to live inside you forever." He began to thrust in earnest, taking me exactly as he had promised.

No, I certainly never dreamt I would lose my virginity to a guy who looks like a vampire gladiator and wants to worship my body like I'm a goddess.

I've lost track of time again as he lies in bed next to me. The only indication any time has passed at all is the changing color of the sky from blue to a fiery orange and now to black. I'm savoring every rise and fall of his chest against my back when I hear my phone ding.

My mom.

Your father and I just got home. Where are you? she texts.

Out, I respond.

Curfew, she reminds me.

I look at the time on my phone, realizing how late it is.

Shit.

I'm an adult, I text back but I know I'm probably pushing it.

But fine. Be home soon.

Ok. And don't worry, we haven't, nor will we, tell your brother. This is your own battle to fight.

I cringe at the thought of having to tell Ethan about Asher but I'm sure I can keep this a secret for the next few months.

"I need to get home," I sigh.

He pulls me in toward him, planting a lingering kiss into the curve of my shoulder.

"Okay, baby, let's go," he says, and we both get up to pull on our clothes.

————

"Are you going to tell me what your tattoo is about?" I ask as the wind whips through my hair. The nighttime air is a cool caress against my skin, and tiny goosebumps snake up my arms and legs. Seeing it again, the intricate black curves and lines and dots, I am curious.

Asher pauses, and I can tell he's still debating whether he's ready to tell me. I'm about to remind him I let him take my virginity today when his voice pierces the silence.

"My biological father. He left my mom and me when I was three, and I've had this plan ever since I was a little kid to get revenge somehow. The tattoo is a sigil. It's supposed to help you manifest your desires. The tattoo artist designed it. Supposedly there's a science behind creating them but I couldn't tell you."

I shouldn't have pried.

"But he's dead now so there goes that plan," Asher says flippantly. "Guess the sigil didn't work."

"Oh," I say, surprised but I understand. I understand how

you can hate another person so deeply, you brand yourself with a permanent reminder of your hate.

"When did he die?"

"I don't know, like a month ago."

I blink, trying to hide my shock.

"Jesus, I'm sorry," I offer.

"I'm not," he says. I can tell he's trying to feign indifference, but the twitching muscle in his jaw gives him away.

"No point in being sad about someone you hated," he says flatly.

I refrain from pointing out he's wrong. I want to apologize for asking about something so personal but decide it's better to leave it alone.

He finds a spot along the side of my street and parks the convertible his stepdad unknowingly loaned us for the day.

"You don't need to walk me to the door," I say as he gets out of the car.

"I'm not."

"Then what are you doing?"

"Coming inside."

"My parents will kill me if they see you."

"Then sneak me in."

I'm giving him a look that says *absolutely not* when he pulls me close to him until we're standing face-to-face.

"Addison," he says quietly, and I wish I could see all the details of his expression through the darkness. "I just spent the last twenty-some-odd hours with you, half of them inside you and the other half thinking about being inside you. Most of my body is covered with your cum and if I close my eyes, I can still taste you in my mouth. The fuck I'm not coming inside with you. If I have to scale the goddamn drainpipe to sleep next to you tonight, I will. But if I'm being honest, my dick is very chafed right now so the front door would be so much easier."

CHAPTER 20

Asher

I'M SMILING AGAIN at how terrified she was when both of us woke up to hear her parents talking downstairs. We had agreed I would leave before dawn but when we failed to wake up in time, I really thought she was going to make me scale the drainpipe after all.

The fear on her face was so goddamn cute.

Obviously we were exhausted. I had meant to keep a tally of her orgasms, but once she went past twelve, I lost count.

Now I'm driving with Wyatt to a return-to-campus barbeque at a different fraternity, which is honestly the last place I want to be. Addison's been on campus for a few days, but I haven't heard much from her. I'm sure she's busy and I find myself wondering, and hoping, her mother was well enough to make the trip. I didn't want to upset her by asking.

Her mother had appeared healthy when she answered their door at seven a.m. – shocked I could tell to find me standing outside and even more shocked when I asked to see Addison – but that was over a week ago and according to Addison, things can change quickly.

This past week, I made the effort of trying to send Addison at least one text a day. After I flew back to New York,

I tried to salvage the remaining time I had left of summer break seeing as I did fuck all after receiving the news of my biological dad's passing.

I need to get my act together. Professor Friedman is going to be pissed at me for not making more progress on my startup this summer.

Since I saw Addison, I've more or less barricaded myself in my room, working at my computer until my vision blurs. Admittedly, it's been hard to focus when all I can think about is her. Often, I'll catch my mind wandering back to the day we spent together, replaying in my mind the feeling of her body. Then something on my computer screen will snap me back to reality, and I'll have to start whatever I was doing all over again.

But my god, her *taste.*

The taste of her sweet juices running down my chin, the gushing wet sound her pussy made as I was driving my fingers inside her, the way she *screamed* my name when she came.

Screamed like I was both her salvation and her undoing.

Screamed as if she had been waiting a millennium for my mercy.

Begged me for more and more until our breaths were so ragged, we could no longer speak.

Begged to taste me.

I told her no, not yet. That day was for her, and there was no way I would allow myself to come unless she was coming alongside me.

But her beautiful lips around my dick did sound pretty enticing at the moment.

"Try not to be such an asshole to these guys," Wyatt says as he parks. The image I have in my head of Addison on her knees pops like a balloon.

"I make no promises," I respond. Wyatt knows how I feel about the tools in this frat. They all suck, and I'd rather pluck out my ball hairs one by one than make conversation with these meatheads. They are an embarrassment to this school, but I guess Harvard needs a football team. Besides, this is exactly why I didn't want to be president of our fraternity and was elated when Wyatt agreed to take the role.

I hate people.

Wyatt shoots me a look.

"Maybe Chloe will be here," he mocks.

"I pray she isn't," I groan.

I still hadn't officially ended things with Chloe, my fling of convenience I bedded far too often last year. The problem is, once my drink count hits double digits and I have a few lines of cocaine under my belt, her ass starts to look like a place I'd like to park my dick for a few hours.

And every time, I curse myself for it.

I do not like her. She is a spiteful, stuck-up bitch and I've fucked enough Chloes in my day to know she is not a fine wine that grows better with age; she's a vapid, callous star-fucker who dreams of the modeling career she'll never have. Instead, she settles for social media slut who posts thirst traps for a living.

We meander through the shithole of a frat to the backyard when Wyatt turns around with the most maniacal grin I've ever seen him give me.

"Guess it's your lucky day, fuck face."

Shit. That can only mean one thing.

Yep, she's right there, practically waiting by the door for me.

I pretend not to see her even though it's painfully obvious she's staring at me. Thankfully she was in the Hamptons the entire summer. Despite my one weekend there, I managed to avoid her for the last three months.

Absolute bliss.

"Hi, stranger," she chirps as she saunters toward me. "Long time no see."

"Chloe," I say. I'm looking at Wyatt like he better bring me a beer immediately, but he just smirks and walks away.

"How was your summer?" she says in an overly sweet voice. "I missed you. You could have texted me, you know."

"Sorry," I say, crossing my arms. "Just really busy with my startup."

She gives me a feline grin. "Could have fooled me based on your social media posts, although I don't doubt you were rather *preoccupied*."

"Asher, buddy!" a familiar male voice says from behind.

I turn around to see Miles. Sweet, sweet Miles.

I met Miles three days into my freshman year, and we were fast friends. If I could have a brother of my choosing, I would pick him. He's good-natured and funny, works decently hard in school, and has no problem keeping me honest. Unlike every other person in my life who either avoids me altogether because I'm a dick or kisses my ass because I'm a dick, Miles does neither. And I love him for it.

"Miles!" I exclaim, turning to give him a bear hug of an embrace. "Good to see you man. I missed you in New York this summer."

"Mind if I steal him from you, Chloe? We have some catching up to do."

"Of course," she sneers, giving Miles the fakest of smiles.

She very much does mind.

"Thank you," I say under my breath as we head toward the kegs and leave a bloodthirsty Chloe behind.

Miles gives boyish chuckle.

"So catch me up," he says while pumping the keg. "What'd I miss?"

I shrug. "Not much, worked on my startup, found out my biological dad died, spiraled."

"Right, sounds like not very much," he says sarcastically. "And Chloe?"

"What about her?"

"Were you with her over the summer?"

"God no."

He gives me an incredulous look. "Then who is the girl-friend Wyatt said you have?"

"Oh…"

Dammit Wyatt.

"Not my girlfriend yet, but I did fuck Ethan's sister."

Miles literally spits out his beer all over my feet and as gross as it is, I start laughing at how casually I just admitted to sleeping with the girl I've been obsessed with for years.

Miles likes to tell me when I get three sheets to the wind drunk, I'll start talking about (no, drooling over) Addison, droning on and on about how beautiful she is, how smart she is, how I would give anything to be with her, how I'm going to have to kill Ethan before he kills me first but it would be worth it because I'm so in love with this girl who barely knows I exist.

"What?!" Miles asks, excited for me like a gossiping schoolgirl. "You did not!"

"I did," I smile triumphantly.

"When?"

"About a week ago. But truthfully our sexual tension had been building all summer. I was with Ethan at the beginning of June and then again during the week of July Fourth, and I saw her both times. Let's just say we had a few…"

I try to think of the right word.

"…encounters. But Ethan was always around so these encounters never achieved their full potential."

"And? So?" Miles says, eagerly awaiting the rest of the story.

"Then like a week ago, I flew out to LA for twenty-four hours and made her scream my name a bunch of times. That's all really." I add a shrug for emphasis.

He throws his head back in a fit of laughter.

"That is definitely not all there is to this little love story of yours but fine. So you fucked her and then what? Are you together? Dating?"

I shake my head. "No, we haven't gotten that far yet. I have no idea where her head's at, but I do need to see her soon. She arrived a few days ago for orientation but I've been waiting for her to text me she's free. I'm assuming she's been busy with her parents."

I don't see Wyatt approaching until I feel the slap of his hand on my shoulder.

"You tell him?" he asks.

"About Addison?" I say.

"Obviously, you fuck, unless there's another girl we don't know about."

"He did tell me," Miles confirms. "And honestly, I'm really proud of our boy here. Wasted no time whatsoever. As soon as Ethan was out of the picture, bam! Makes his move."

"Better keep it under wraps, though," Wyatt says. "King Ethan still has eyes here, and any number of these fucks would run and tell him in a heartbeat."

"And if Chloe doesn't stab you with an icepick when she finds out you've moved on," Wyatt continues, "Ethan sure as shit will."

"I know," I mutter. "I'm a dead man."

"Might want to start digging your grave now," Miles comments under his breath as I turn to see Chloe marching toward me.

CHAPTER 21

Addison

"YOU'RE ALSO AB LIKE ME!"

I turn to see the first smiling face I've seen since setting foot in the Sciences quad. So far, everyone here looks downright miserable.

Not only is she smiling, she's stunning.

The first thing I notice is perfect, almond-shaped eyes framed by long, jet-black lashes.

"I'm Addison," I say, extending a hand.

"Anjali," she says in return, giving my hand a polite shake.

I fish out the orientation packet for my major and step aside so she can do the same.

"I'm so nervous about biology," she says. "Did you know the dropout rate for that class is over fifty percent?"

I didn't but I do now.

"Yikes," I wince. "So, you're saying it's going to be a blast?"

"Ha! Most definitely. And at eight a.m. three days a week. What could be more fun?"

"What dorm are you in?" Anjali asks.

"Hollis. You?" I respond.

"Wait, stop! I'm also in Hollis! What floor?"

"Fourth."

"I'm on the third floor. How are your suitemates?"

"Um, I'm in a single."

"WHAT?! How did you swing that?!" Anjali gasps.

"I… I don't know. That's just where they put me. It's nice but also, I wish I had suitemates. It would be nice to have some friends."

"You mean forced friends with someone who probably has poor hygiene? No thanks. Consider yourself blessed."

"You can be my friend," she says as she turns to me and smiles.

"Do you have poor hygiene?" I tease.

"Do I *look* like I have poor hygiene?"

Fair. Not with those perfectly white teeth.

"What's your story?" she asks. "Where are you from? What do you want to do when you graduate? Do you have a boyfriend? That sort of thing."

I haven't been asked so many questions about myself in a long time.

"Los Angeles, ideally research – either vaccine development or cancer research, no boyfriend. You?"

"Bay Area, probably research although I'm still debating PhD versus MD."

"Med school, wow. Very different," I comment.

"Very different for sure. Oh, no boyfriend either, but not opposed!"

My phone dings, and I look down to see a text from Asher.

When can I see you? it says.

"Worried parents?" Anjali asks.

"Um, no, it's just this guy I know who goes here."

Her eyes light up. "Do we like this guy? Is he cute?"

I laugh. "He's cute, in my opinion."

"And do you like him?"

"I don't know… maybe?"

"Ha!" she laughs. "Maybe is a no. How do you know him?"

"He's my brother's friend and also from LA."

"Scandalous! Does your brother know?"

"There's nothing to know, really," I say.

I don't know why I'm lying to her, but it seems less risky than telling someone I met five minutes ago my life story.

Whenever, I text back.

Now?

I'm walking back to my dorm.

Can I not meet you there?

Sure, I guess. Hollis 406.

"He's like insisting on seeing me," I scoff.

"It sounds like there is *a lot* more to tell," she grins. "It's okay," she continues as she fluffs her hair. "We just met. I don't expect you to spill all your secrets just yet, but you must know I will soon expect to hear details."

"When are you seeing him?" she asks.

She sounds as boy crazy as I feel.

"He said he wants to meet me at my dorm."

Her eyes go wide. "Can I see him?!"

I must be giving her a funny look because she immediately says, "Is that weird?"

"No, it's fine," I chuckle. "Besides, you can tell me later if he's actually cute or not. And I can show you where my room is."

"Right, your *single.* And you thought you wanted suitemates. Good luck bringing a guy back to a quad with three other roommates!"

———

We round the corner, and Anjali snatches my elbow, yanking me to a halt. I almost yelp in pain when she whispers, "ADDISON, there is the most gorgeous man I have ever seen standing in your hallway."

I look up and lay eyes on said gorgeous man.

"That's him," I say quietly, and her eyes go wide in disbelief. No wonder this man has such a horribly inflated sense of self.

Asher's lazily leaning against my doorframe, fingers scrolling through his phone and oblivious to the bustling bodies and gawking onlookers passing him in the hallway. It's not until we're a handful of feet in front of him that he looks up, taking me in with that cocky grin he likes to wear.

"Hi," I say, doing my best not to cower under his unfaltering confidence. "This is Anjali. She's in my major."

"Hi," Anjali says sweetly, giving him a wave.

"Asher," he says back, yet to move from his tilted perch.

An awkward moment passes, and I find myself annoyed Asher isn't making more of an effort.

"Well, let's meet up later, Addison?" Anjali asks, sensing Asher's lack of patience. I want to apologize on his behalf for acting so disinterested and rude.

"Sounds great, I'll text you," I say, giving her the warmest smile I can muster. She's the first normal person I've met since arriving on campus, and I don't want to blow this opportunity to make a friend.

She gives me a subtle wave, and I do the same before turning around to unlock the door. The lock opens and I give Asher a *"what is your problem?"* glare as he saunters past me into my closet-sized room.

"Wow, a single," he says as I shut the door. "How did you swing that, I wonder?"

"Honestly, I have no idea. This is just where they put me."

"My princess needs her privacy," Asher smirks, and I'm

struck with the odd notion that my luck obtaining a single may not have been luck whatsoever.

A question forms at my lips but before I can say anything, he pulls me between his legs now dangling off the edge of my bed.

"God, I've missed you," he whispers into my mouth as our tongues dance together.

A soft whimper escapes my lips as I kiss him greedily, allowing myself to acknowledge the feelings I've repressed since I last saw him. That day we spent together didn't feel real. Falling asleep next to him in my bed must have been my imagination. It was too good, too perfect – there had to be a catch.

His hand snakes down my backside until the width of his palm is firmly planted against my ass and he tugs me upward so I can straddle him. We're balanced in a precarious position on the edge of my bed, and the friction of my jean shorts against my clit as he hardens under me draws a breathy moan from my mouth.

I did not expect my need for him to be so overwhelming.

I push into his chest, and he lays back on the flimsy material calling itself a mattress. He repositions both of us so we're no longer seconds away from sliding off. I strip off my own clothes this time, pulling my shirt over my head to reveal a regrettably everyday bra, which I quickly unhook and toss to the floor. I grab the base of his T-shirt, but he does the rest of the work, pulling at the collar to slide it over his head.

We're writhing against each other now, shirtless but clothed from the waist down. I watch his eyes take in the sight of my breasts beneath his roaming fingers, and his thumbs brush over my nipples as they sharpen to rock-hard peaks. I'm still grinding on top of him, the inseam of my shorts now doing wonders to heighten my arousal.

Our eyes meet, although I find it hard to keep mine open.

"Take these off," he orders, nearly ripping my shorts in

half as he pulls apart the top button and zipper. I have to slide off the bed to fully undress myself, which he uses as an opportunity to pull off his shorts and fish a condom out of his pocket.

I watch him unroll it down himself. His pace is perfectly sufficient, yet I find it frustratingly unhurried. I straddle him again, impatient, as I peer down to guide him inside me.

I release a groan as his girth pushes my walls apart, toeing that edge between pleasure and pain I recently discovered I so desperately enjoy. *God, it hurt. It hurt in a way that felt so fucking good and I never wanted it to stop.*

Both of us pant uncontrollably, our voices hushed given the thin walls of the surrounding dorm room. I can't stop myself from sliding down on him harder and faster, driving him deeper inside me until my fingertips start to tingle.

"Slow down," he whispers, looking down to watch himself slide in and out of my opening.

I don't.

He throws his head back against my pillow, squeezing his eyelids closed. "Slow down, Addison, or I'm going to come," he begs.

"Stop talking," I say between gasps, refusing to compromise as I arch my back into my thrusts. I feel his thumb begin to rub my clit and I know what he's doing, getting me closer to my edge because he refuses to come before me.

The familiar clenching sensation I feel in my stomach as my climax draws near overpowers all my other senses. I close my eyes, focusing only on the pressure of him inside me. The caress of his thumb causes my inner thighs to quiver, and I'm suspended in time. I only hear the sound of my breathing – one breath, two, three – before the quiver gives way to a violent spasm and my release crashes through me like a torrential downpour.

Slowly I come to a stop, working to steady my breath. I

can still feel him inside me, and I realize I have no idea if he has also finished.

"Did you come?" My voice is breathy as I open my eyes to find his gaze.

"Of course I came," he responds, equally out of breath. "Did you not... never mind," he pants, closing his eyes.

"Never mind, what?" I ask.

His eyes open again to meet mine. "Never mind, I forgot we are still using condoms," he answers.

"Why would we not use condoms?"

"You're on the pill, aren't you?" he asks.

"I have an IUD," I say. "But I want to be careful."

"I know, baby," he says, lifting me off him.

I will never get used to the feeling of him sliding out of me and how his absence immediately triggers a longing to have him back. I release a breath I didn't even realize I was holding, and it sounds a lot like an irritated sigh.

I hear him throw the condom in the wastebasket, and then he lies back down beside me holding his phone above his face. The two of us barely fit on the mattress and I'm forced to lay sideways with the wall pressing into my back to accommodate all six-foot-four of him.

I watch his screen as he types the letters "*v i b r a t o r*" into the search bar.

"What are you doing?" I ask in surprise.

"Buying you a vibrator," he responds matter-of-factly.

"*Why*?"

"In case you get this level of horny again and I'm not around to immediately satiate you."

I laugh at how preposterous that sounds. "I'm not going to fuck some random guy across the hall just because I'm horny and you're momentarily busy."

"I'm not taking any chances."

"You're ridiculous. You don't need to buy me a vibrator," I protest but I can see he's already completed the purchase.

"You have needs, princess," he says, putting his phone down and turning on his side to face me. "And who am I to deny you of your needs simply because I'm not nearby? Besides, I'm looking forward to showing you how to use it on yourself."

A devious grin spreads across his face, and he says in that low, melodic voice of his, "I promise I'm a very hands-on teacher."

CHAPTER 22

Addison

I'M PISSED at the amount of time I spent in bed with Asher today. Classes haven't even started, and I already feel so behind. A thought pops into my mind that I cannot let this thing with Asher become a regular occurrence. I know I had felt differently a few weeks ago, when I abandoned my plan to pursue a gap year so I could be with him, but I will have absolutely no chance whatsoever of surviving this semester, let alone making it into the top five percent of my class, if I'm fucking him every five seconds.

I need to get myself under control. Maybe the vibrator is a good idea after all.

As I had promised, I text Anjali to see if she's around. She immediately texts back asking if I want to join her for dinner in the dining hall.

"I'm so sorry I was so awkward earlier," she says as soon as we find each other in the courtyard.

"What are you talking about?" I ask.

"In front of Asher. He's so hot, Addison, I forgot how to form sentences."

"Well, don't tell him he's hot. He already has a massive ego. Plus, you weren't being awkward. He was being rude."

"He's just so… *intimidating*," she says, still awestruck.

"He's definitely a vibe," I agree. "He has a reputation for being an asshole."

"Is he an asshole to you?" she asks with concern.

"No. At least not yet," I joke. I savor the thought of how differently he treats me, like a princess on a pedestal.

"So what's the deal with you two then?" she pries. "You said you didn't have a boyfriend."

"I don't. Honestly, I'm not sure," I shrug. "We hooked up a few times over the summer but nothing serious. And then about a week ago, he flew out to LA. Oh, I should have mentioned he was living in New York over the summer. And we had this crazy twenty-four hours."

"Like, *crazy, crazy?*" she asks, practically drooling, which makes me laugh. *I really like this girl. I hope we stay friends.*

"I'm not a virgin," she interjects before I can confirm or deny the amount of crazy. "So you don't need to hold back on my account. In fact, please do not hold back. If anything, embellish."

I'm grinning like a fool. "He… We…," I pause, trying to find the right words to describe our fuck-fest without sounding crass. "We basically had sex nonstop for twenty-four hours."

"And it was incredible," I add. "Actually, it was the most incredible twenty-four hours I've ever had in my life."

"WOW," Anjali's eyes are wide with excitement. "So he's like in love with you?"

This causes me to laugh again. "I'd hardly say he's in love with me. Also, I hardly even know him. I mean, I've known him for years but always as my brother's friend, so his recent attention has all been very… sudden. I have no idea what he's thinking or what he wants."

"But I'm trying not to get too carried away," I admit. "I'm so nervous about this semester. I really, really want to make it into the top five percent to get invited to the summer fellowship program. It was one of the reasons I came here."

"Girl, you and me both," Anjali laments. "This semester is going to kick our asses. We are going to get destroyed."

"God, it's going to be terrible," I say. "Even more of a reason I can't let Asher consume me. I've already been obsessing over him way too much as it is."

"Just have fun then," Anjali says, as if turning off one's emotions is easy. "Plus, you'll have me to keep you accountable."

"Let's say a prayer of thanks to the universe for bringing us together and then shove this disgusting chicken in our pie holes so we can finish the pre-work for bio tomorrow," she says.

Ugh, right. Pre-work.

We already have a homework assignment due before eight a.m. tomorrow – an assignment I likely would have already finished this afternoon if it weren't for the distraction of a certain devastatingly handsome someone.

Fuck.

CHAPTER 23

Asher

"ARE you ready to start the pilot trials?" Professor Friedman asks.

"Almost," I answer.

"But you were *almost* ready at the end of last semester."

I knew he'd be up my ass about my lack of progress this summer. As my mentor, he has every right to call me on my shit. I fucked up badly.

"I know," I say. "Completing the user interface beta took more development time than I expected." In my defense, it's true, but I should still be lightyears farther along.

He gives me a deservedly disappointed look.

"You can't afford to fall behind this semester with your startup, Asher."

"I know," I say again. "I won't."

I curl and uncurl my fingers into a fist to suppress the bubble of anger rising in my throat. If I weren't in my professor's office, I might have put a hole through the wall.

What the fuck is wrong with me?

"You'll lock up when you leave?" Professor Friedman asks. It's not unusual for me to work late in his office, away from the distractions and noise of the frat house. But right now the silence is deafening.

"Of course," I say. "Have a good night."

He gives me a nod and I swear his eyes are telling me, *"you better not fuck this up."*

Dammit, I hate myself right now.

I wring the frustration from my eyes with the heel of my palm and try again to focus, which conveniently reminds me I need to text Addison.

Your present has arrived, I text. *When can I use it on you?*

I'm annoyed at how lackluster her communication has been but I'm also not sure what I was expecting. I'm equally guilty and haven't bothered to text her since we were last together. I wasn't intentionally avoiding her. I just… *was busy.*

Three days ago, after my reckoning about how woefully behind I truly was with my startup, I locked myself in my room and went on a development bender. No one bothered me, until Thursday night rolled around and everyone was headed out to the bars. By that time, I figured it might be productive to let off some steam.

It was not.

Wyatt and I are horrible influences on each other and should be forbidden from doing cocaine together. He turns into a raging lunatic who can't stop running his mouth, and apparently I turn into a werewolf.

It's so fun though.

It's a dopamine rush to become the most obnoxious version of your alter ego. For me, that alter ego is evil incarnate. When I'm in one of my… *moods*, when my grip on reality is so completely altered and under the influence, I find myself wishing some dickhead would give me one reason to send a man to the hospital. I'm the living embodiment of fuck around and find out.

Miles tells me I have repressed anger issues I need to deal with. But the way I see it, someone needs to play the villain in this fucked up life, so why not me? For the record, not that anyone disputes this, I'm quite good at it – a natural born asshole.

I decide enough time has passed since Professor Friedman left, and I pack up my laptop. I shouldn't leave. *I should sit my ass down and work.* But I have a more pressing matter: Addison needs her present.

———

I'm rather annoyed by the amount of cajoling it takes to pry Addison from her beloved library. But she caves at last, and I'm now patiently waiting for her in the parking lot.

"Hi," she says as she climbs in my beloved G-Wagen.

"Where's your stuff?" I ask in confusion.

"In the library," she says. I sense aggravation in her tone.

"I'm confused," I say. "You're going back in there?"

"You said you had something for me so I came to get it."

"Oh no, princess. I do have something for you but it requires a bit of *instruction.*"

She looks at me with pursed lips.

"I mean, we certainly could do our lesson in there," I motion toward the library. "But it's not the most welcoming place for you to scream my name. I'm up for the challenge though."

"I have to go back tonight, Asher. I have a quiz tomorrow and I need to prepare."

I look at her incredulously.

"I'm sorry," she whines. "Asher, this major is so hard. I'm in way over my head and I already feel beyond stressed."

"You know, the present I have for you can help with that."

"I'm serious, Asher."

"Fine," I concede, "I'll just take you for a drive then. How much time can you spare?"

"Forty-five minutes. An hour, tops."

I roll my neck in frustration but I suppose I can make it work.

"Let me just text Anjali and tell her," she says as I start the ignition.

I reach for the gift bag on the floor of the backseat and hand it to her.

"For you," I say, and she sorts through the tissue paper, pulling out a rectangular box.

"Oh my god," she snorts, and I steal glimpses of her opening the package. The curiosity with which she studies the sex toy amuses me.

"I guess I thought it would be bigger," she smirks.

"Why would I get you one bigger than I am?" I laugh.

"Do they make them that big?" she quips with feigned sincerity, causing a garish smile to spread across my face.

"You flatter me, princess," I grin.

"Where are you taking me?" she asks, surveying the passing surroundings.

"A quiet place I like to go when I need to clear my head."

Another ten minutes pass, and I park my car on the outskirts of a woodland area. I've come here before when I want to clear my head. It's secluded and at this time of year, the tree leaves have started their annual transformation from lush green to hues of gold, orange and red.

I unbuckle my seatbelt. "Get out, we're getting in the back."

She narrows her eyes.

"You said you were stressed baby girl," I reason. "So we're going to un-stress you."

Reluctantly, she opens the passenger door and joins me in the back of the car. I always forget how narrow the backseat is. You'd think the back seat of a G-Wagen would be bigger based on how the car looks from the outside but nope, far too small to maneuver as easily as I would like.

"Take your pants off," I say as I unzip mine, coaxing

myself a bit as I watch her undress. Her small frame has a much easier time navigating the cramped space.

"Straddle me," I tell her. She looks at me with reservation, but it's not a question.

"I know your body's not ready yet," I say, assuring here there will be a warmup. "We're going to get you there."

"No, the other way," I say as she climbs on top of my lap to face me. "Turn around."

She slithers her body around, successfully getting a knee on either side of mine and I pull her back against my chest so she's forced into a lean.

"You're very stiff," I say, taking her hand in mine as I snake both of our fingers down her front.

Our fingers part the folds of her pussy, and I reposition my hand on top of hers as I slide her first two fingers further down until we land on her opening.

"There, baby," I say, reassuring her she's in the right spot as I kiss the side of her neck. I pulse her two fingers in and out with mine.

"Do you feel yourself getting wet?" I ask, keeping my voice as calm and soothing as possible.

She nods. "Yes," she says, her voice getting breathy.

"Are you wet enough for me yet?"

"I don't know," she swallows.

"The answer is no, you're not."

My hand starts to get greedy, needing to fondle her, to press inside her, but I school myself to hold back.

"Finger yourself," I whisper, and I guide her two fingers inside her opening as her breath hitches. I relinquish my hand, tucking it under her sweatshirt instead to find her nipple and gently twist it into a hard point. A delicate moan escapes her lips as she begins to writhe against her own fingers, drawing out her pleasure.

"Good girl," I tell her as the heat of her arousal begins to fog the windows. My erection is hard against her back, and I slip my fingers between her again. *She's ready.*

"Sit up," I say and help her position herself so her opening hovers right above my dick before guiding myself inside her.

She gasps loudly as she throws her head back, moaning now as she slowly bounces herself up and down, every muscle in her legs working overtime.

I grip the skin of her outer thighs, digging my fingertips into her soft, supple flesh. I love when she's loud like this, unrestrained and feral.

I dig my heels into the floor and thrust my pelvis upward in sync with her downward bounce. My cock reaches so deep inside her, it elicits a scream. I see her fingertips threatening to pierce holes in the leather headrest of the driver's seat, which only makes me want to thrust harder.

"Tell me to fuck you harder," I say, panting for breath.

"Fuck me harder," she yells.

"Say my name," I growl. "Fuck me harder, *Asher*," I correct her, squeezing her skin hard enough to hurt.

"Fuck me harder, Asher," she screams in obedience.

I allow her to enjoy two more thrusts of pressure before I take her hand again in mine and bring her fingertips down to her clit.

"Here, baby," I command, guiding her fingers underneath mine to trace tiny circles around her bud, applying just the right amount of pressure I know she needs to coax out her release.

Her breath is ragged, and she chokes down air as her moans crescendo.

"I want you to make yourself come," I grunt. I would give anything for a mirror right now so I could watch her fondle herself into oblivion, following my instructions like the good girl she is. I press my head back against the seat so I can take in more of her backside as it grinds on top of me.

My moans now match hers in intensity as we pound

against each other. She is so close now, I can practically smell her orgasm.

"*Harder, harder,*" she screams, and I nearly pull a hamstring as I feel her cum soak through my pants at the same time as I empty inside her.

She gasps for air as the thrusts stop. Her head leans against the hand she's still using to death grip the back of the seat in front of her, and I watch the rise and fall of her back as she steadies herself.

I pull her into my chest as I wrap an arm around her, kissing the curve of her neck.

Her other hand is still resting between her legs, and I bring it up to my mouth as I wrap my tongue around her first two fingers, sucking on them like a lollipop.

Our comingled slickness covers my crotch and my god is it a beautiful feeling. Her orgasm. My seed. Together.

My lips part and I barely come to my senses in time to stop myself from telling her I love her. The realization of what I almost said sends my heart racing. The words are stuck in my throat and swallowing them down slices me raw. I have to suppress an overwhelming urge to start crying. I *can't* say those words to her yet. I'm not ready.

I'm not ready to let these feelings see the light of day – not yet – and this truth feels like a knife to the chest. My windpipe constricts at the panic of what I almost said, and I need to get her off me, urgently.

I move her as gently and casually as I can, but she's looking at me like something very, very wrong just happened.

Shit, did I actually tell her I love her out loud?

She's curled up into herself across from me in the backseat.

"Are you okay?" I ask, and she looks like she's going to cry.

"You didn't use a condom," she whispers.

That's an issue?

"I'm sorry," I say, although I don't really understand. She said she has an IUD and, I've been inside her at least three dozen times already. It feels right.

"Did you not like the feeling of it?" I ask. Her distressed reaction to my sperm inside her disappoints me more than it should.

"I wasn't ready."

"Okay," I say, trying to keep the derision out of my tone. "I don't have STDs if that's what you're concerned about."

"It's more than that," she says.

I want to press further but it occurs to me she's still half-naked in my backseat, and I'm still sitting here with my dick out.

"It won't happen again," I say apologetically. "Not until you're ready."

She reaches for her clothes, and I hate this is how our drive is ending.

"Hey," I say, reaching for her to pull her mouth onto mine. "I am sorry. I got carried away and you're right, you didn't give me permission to take you without a condom."

"It's okay," she says softly, kissing me back. "Let's just be more careful next time."

"Speaking of next time, when can I teach you how to use your new toy? Tomorrow?"

"This weekend," she counters. "Sorry, I just have a ton of work to get through."

"Did you not have this much work when you were a freshman?" she asks, and I'm embarrassed to admit I spent most of my freshman year drunk and doing lines of cocaine with her brother.

"Not like you do. My major is not as demanding."

"Must be nice."

"Not as nice as watching you make yourself come." I can't help myself.

"Well, don't get used to it. I like it better when you do it," she retorts.

"You say that now but just wait until I make you use that new toy of yours. I'm worried once you go vibrator, you'll never go back."

She grins, rolling her eyes at me in a way that makes me certain I want to be the only one she rolls her eyes at for the rest of our lives.

And that terrifies me.

CHAPTER 24

Addison

"ARE you sure you don't want to text him?" Anjali asks me. It's ten-thirty p.m. on our third Saturday since arriving on campus, and Anjali has declared we're going out.

"Anjali, is it terrible I want to stay in tonight?" I ask.

"Listen, we've been busting our asses since day one," she reminds me.

"Before day one, actually," I reluctantly agree.

"Yes! Before day one," she agrees.

"We deserve, nay we *need*, to get blackout drunk and meet other people."

"Specifically boys?" I smile.

"Not all of us can be so lucky, Addison, to have our own personal sex god."

"Have you ever been to his frat?" she asks. "Seems like he's always coming here."

"Never," I admit. "But aren't frats gross? And also why would I want to do a walk of shame?"

"Trust me, there is *no shame* in fucking that man," she adds with emphasis. "I don't know why you aren't parading him around campus, screaming it from the rooftops."

"Because I don't have time," I say.

"Oh please," Anjali says, "I'm sure you could spare a few minutes during daytime hours to hang out. Have you ever even gotten lunch together or coffee?"

"No," I say.

"Not even coffee?"

I shake my head. Anjali's right. Why aren't we at least grabbing a coffee together? It feels like we don't talk for days at a time until he resurfaces, begging me to let him come over.

"Is that weird?" I ask her, suddenly self-conscious about our lack of doing relationship things.

"Kinda," she admits. I can tell by the look on her face she wants to say more but is holding back.

"Do you think...," she stops herself. "Is this why you don't want to text him before going to the party tonight at his frat? Because if I were you, I would absolutely be leveraging any connection I have to get us in the door. These parties are notoriously shit shows and are always *packed*."

"What do you mean 'is this why I don't want to text him'?" I ask, trying to stifle the nausea now rolling around in my gut.

"Never mind," she says, sensing my angst. "Forget I said anything. Let's just go and have fun. I'm sure we'll run into him, and he'll be over the moon to see you."

I swallow, acutely aware of my paranoia.

Maybe this is a bad idea.

"What time is it?" Anjali asks as she looks at her phone. "Let's pregame a bit more, then head out. Bottoms up!" she says in my direction, raising her cup of tepid liquid to cheers mine.

"Ugh, disgusting," she grunts.

"You made them, not me," I laugh.

———

Once we arrive at the frat party, I understand immediately what Anjali meant by shit show. It was chaos at the door as a mob of students tried to push their way to the front, hoping to earn the coveted nod of approval from the guy at the door posing as a bouncer.

You would think by the frenzy unfolding in front of us this was the most elite nightclub on campus. Thankfully, Anjali was up for the challenge and shoved her way to the front like a linebacker on steroids. *I've never been prouder.*

We were granted admittance easily, and I tried not to let this superficial accomplishment go to my head.

Anjali continued her beeline, and after narrowly avoiding an elbow or two to the head, we finally found the alcohol.

Kegs. Great.

Anjali hands me a frothy plastic cup of piss water. "Chug it!" she barks. *Whatever does the trick, I guess.*

I scan the room for Asher – nothing yet – and I'm not sure if I'm relieved or more nervous. My heart is beating as if it's going to leap out of my chest, and I have to stop myself from looking for him.

Oh, this is bad. This is a red flag, I can feel it.

It's so loud inside, I fail to notice a random boy who's engaged poor Anjali in conversation. To my dismay, I think I hear her flirting back.

"Do you want to get more beer?" I say to Anjali, practically yelling to make my voice heard over the music.

"That'd be great," she says and hands me her empty cup.

No, that's not what I... oh, whatever, FINE.

I make my way back over to the keg, which now has a line. I'm mortified by the thought of Asher seeing me standing alone, waiting in line for beer. Thank god the queue moves quickly so I can rush back over to the safety of Anjali as soon as possible.

I hand Anjali the beer, and she says something into the ear

of the random guy before grabbing my hand and pulling me onto the dance floor.

I am not drunk enough for this party, I think, making a mental note to pregame more before our next outing.

The dance floor is a mosh pit of drunk, smelly frat boys and girls wearing heinous amounts of perfume. Anjali signals to me with a flip of her finger to chug our beers again so we can ditch the hazardous waste before it sloshes all over us.

I'm praying to the gods to make this second beer kick in as fast as possible when I see Asher. He's perched on an overly wide staircase with the rest of the vultures, all looking like they're scanning the mob for their next meal. That's when I see *her*.

I had been so fixated on him, I didn't see the platinum blonde standing by his side. As I watch, she turns into him like she's going to…

My eyes go wide.

…kiss him. No, not kiss him, fucking making out with him. And he's not pushing her away! He's kissing her back.

Anjali catches my stare and looks in the direction of my gaze only to turn back around in slow motion with a look of horror on her face. Clearly she sees what I do.

Both of our jaws are practically on the floor as she swivels her head back around just in time to see the blonde girl *lead him up the stairs.*

And he's following her to god knows where to do god knows what.

Oh no. Oh no, no, no.

Anjali whips her head back around to me. Although I see her trying to talk to me, I'm frozen. The frenzy of surrounding noises is now so muffled, I feel like I'm in a vacuum. All the air has been sucked from my lungs, and I can't breathe.

I clutch my throat, gasping.

I feel and hear nothing other than the pressure of a hand on my arm yanking me through the throng of bodies. Farther and farther we push, the dim colors of clothing swirling in a blur around me.

I feel like I'm having an out of body experience – like I'm watching a video of myself see the guy I've been sleeping with for the past month, who I let take my virginity, who I let tell me story after story of *lies, of promises,* who I let *fuck me without a condom,* make out with another girl *in public,* in front of *hundreds of people,* then walk upstairs with this same girl, looking at her like he's about to take her to bed…

I was starting to believe this man was *in love with me. IN LOVE WITH ME.*

Was any of it ever fucking real?

I collapse onto a patch of grass outside, gulping in oxygen and violently shaking as a gentle hand, which I pray belongs to Anjali, rubs my back.

And then I throw up.

CHAPTER 25

Addison

IT'S BEEN APPROXIMATELY ten days since my world shattered to pieces.

I've ignored every text and call from him. I've practically moved out of my dorm room and now shack up with Anjali most nights. During the day, if I'm not in class, I'm holed up in the most obscure corner of the library with no cell service.

I look in the mirror and I don't know who I am anymore.

Six nights after I saw him with the blonde girl, I finally managed to *not* cry myself to sleep, which felt like a huge accomplishment. In reality, it was probably my body's way of telling me I was morbidly dehydrated.

"You have to confront him," Anjali keeps telling me. But I can't. I'm mortified I let myself believe Asher Aves wanted anything more from me than sex. How stupid I was.

Stupid, stupid girl.

To him, we were never that serious. In fact, to him, there was no "us," there was only Asher's penis and my maidenhood.

I should have known better. Guys like Asher don't fall for girls like me – they fall for girls like *her*. I haven't learned who she is yet, but I imagine she's some confident and charming social media model, not some mousey, inexperienced, hope-less girl like me.

Maybe I would be more like her if I hadn't had a knife held to my throat when I fifteen by a piece of shit loser who was hell-bent on raping me before I kicked him in the balls and ran away.

I hadn't thought of Connor or what he did since I got here. Because of Asher's promise, I hadn't needed to.

Now, what happened in the girls' bathroom that day is all I can think about.

Connor took that from me – my chance of becoming like *her*. Maybe if he hadn't tried to rape me, turning me into a shell of myself, I would have spent my formative high school years flourishing. I would be the kind of brash, charismatic girl who can lead a boy upstairs like a dog on a leash. But I was not given the chance to become that girl. I was too busy trying and failing to put the splintered pieces of myself back together. And now, here I am, heartbroken, crying my fucking eyes out, over a boy who never did and never will give a shit about me.

No, I cannot and will not confront him.

If I do, it will only end in humiliation. I can picture the scene in my head: me, confronting Asher, and him awkwardly telling me he only ever wanted to be friends with benefits.

Anjali and I are walking down the sidewalk when I hear my name.

"ADDISON."

Both Anjali and I whip around.

Fuck.

"Addison!" Asher jogs toward us, arriving out of breath. I glance over at Anjali, who's giving him a look that says *take one more step toward her and I gut you.*

"I've been trying to get a hold of you for almost two weeks. Where've you been? Are you okay? Did you get sick? Did your mom get sick? I was getting really worried, Addison. I stopped by your room several times, but you weren't there. I thought something terrible happened to you."

Something terrible DID happen to me.

"I'm fine," I say curtly.

"Okay…," he says with confusion. "Is something going on?"

"No," I shrug.

"Okay, well, that's bullshit."

"It's not *bullshit*, I've just been *busy*, Asher. The world doesn't always revolve around you, you know?"

The venom drips off my tongue thick as honey, and he looks at me like I've lost my mind.

"Can we talk for a second?"

I contemplate saying no but admittedly, I'm curious to hear what lies he will spin this time.

"Sure," I say, crossing my arms.

He looks at me and then looks at Anjali.

"Alone?" he asks.

I look over at Anjali, and her wide eyes say *do not give him the time of day.*

"Actually, we have to get to class. Maybe another time."

We both turn to walk away when that *asshole* grabs my arm, *hard,* and yanks me around to face him. I swear Anjali was a split second away from landing a right hook across his jaw.

"Just give us a second," he barks at Anjali and drags me three steps backwards.

"What the fuck is going on with you?" he says under his breath, searching my eyes for an answer.

I have trouble looking at him and can feel the telltale sting of tears building in my eyes.

"Let me go," I breathe through my clenched teeth, refusing to make direct eye contact.

"Did I do something?" he asks, as if he doesn't know the answer. *Playing dumb.*

"Listen," he says, his voice low. "I'm *sorry* about the condom thing last time."

Ohhhhhh, buddy, that was the WRONG thing to say.

I look at him now, seething. I almost raise my hand to slap him, but the bustle of students walking past us jolts some sense into me. This is not the time or place for this conversation.

"Asher," I say in a hushed, serious voice. "I am going through *a lot* right now and I need you to give me some *fucking space.*"

He drops my arm as a flicker of hurt passes over his face.

"Okay," he croaks as the strained bob of his throat tries to force down a swallow.

I give him one last glare as if to mark him, before I pivot and rejoin Anjali who's waiting anxiously a few feet away.

CHAPTER 26

Asher

"SOMEONE'S IN A MOOD," Wyatt says as I rejoin my friends at lunch. From the window, I had seen Addison and her friend walking and had literally sprung out of my seat to run after her.

I don't think I've ever run after a woman in my life.

I glare at Wyatt before sitting back down.

"Everything okay?" Miles asks.

"He's been pissy like this for the last few weeks," Wyatt mumbles.

"I can fucking hear you, dickhead," I snap.

"Has our resident Icarus finally flown too close to the sun?" Jaxon asks snidely.

"Girl troubles if I had to guess," Wyatt says to Jaxon as if I'm not sitting directly across from him. My patience over these last few weeks has grown precariously thin, and I worry something inconsequential, like the conversation happening across from me now, will crack whatever remaining hold I have on my rage.

"Chloe?" I hear Jaxon ask.

Wyatt shakes his head.

I look up to see the wheels furiously turning in Jaxon's pea brain, then he looks at me with his knowing weasel grin.

"Asher," Jaxon starts, and I know from his tone, he's figured it out. "Why were you chasing down Ethan's sister outside? And why, after presumably speaking with her, do you look like you've had a fight with a hornet's nest and lost?"

I say nothing and pretend to be interested in my food, although after the encounter with Addison, I've lost my appetite.

"Oh my god. You're fucking her, aren't you?"

"For how long?" Jaxon squeals. "Does Ethan know?"

"Of course, Ethan doesn't know, and I know, Jaxon, that you're Ethan's bitch but if you say a fucking word to him, I will rip out each of your fingernails."

Jaxon cackles like a toddler. "Oh my god, that's ripe. Not only are you fucking Ethan's sister, but you're two-timing her with Chloe!"

"I'm not two-timing her with Chloe," I sneer.

"Liar. You two were making out in front of everyone at the party a few weeks ago!"

I swear I'm going to give this kid a black eye if he doesn't shut up.

"Did you sleep with her?" Jaxon asks.

This guy just won't let it go.

"No."

"But?"

"Asher, don't lie to us. You were out of your mind that night. You slept with her again, didn't you?"

"No!" I protest. "I didn't. But she might have sucked my dick, and I might have fingered her, I don't know."

I feel nothing but blistering shame as I say the truth aloud.

"ASHER!" Wyatt scolds me. "What the fuck is wrong with you? You need to get your shit together. That should say a lot coming from me, who's practically a walking disaster."

I wince. He's right.

"I fucked up! I know! I was drunk and high and Chloe was just… around!"

I feel immense regret as those words leave my mouth.

"Yeah but Asher, you can't tell Chloe you only want to be friends on Tuesday and then hook up with her Saturday. It sends a mixed signal!" Wyatt exclaims. "She's going to think you like her, and I know you don't!"

"I'm with Wyatt on this one," Miles chimes in.

"You could bring Addison around, you know?" Miles says.

"Yeah but then she would get caught in Chloe's crossfire, and I don't want that for her," I say.

"See, your logic is a bit flawed here," Miles continues. "You don't want to hook up with Chloe, but she's around. But you won't bring Addison around because you don't want her to bear the wrath of Chloe's jealousy. So because you won't bring Addison around, you end up right back where you started and hook up with Chloe. You do see the error in your ways, right?"

"I know, *I know*," I groan. "I've been obsessed with this girl for years and now she's finally here and I've managed to royally fuck it up. She won't even talk to me right now. I can't get her to return so much as a text message."

"How did she find out about Chloe?" Miles asks.

"She doesn't know about Chloe," I say. "I don't know what's going on with her."

"Maybe she's just not that into you," Jaxon smirks. "I know rejection is foreign to you, Asher, but perhaps she's met someone else and wants you to just… oh I don't know, leave her the fuck alone!"

"I want you to know I am five fucking seconds away from slapping that grin off your face with my goddamn fist," I curse at Jaxon.

"Okay, easy, *easy*," Wyatt says, trying to bring down the temperature at the table.

"Asher, let's go to the gym," Miles says, standing. "I think you need to work off some steam."

———

I'm sorry for earlier, I text Addison. *I promise I'll give you space but I need to know you're okay. I don't feel good about how we left things.*

I'm fine, she texts back.

I rack my brain for the right words to say.

I understand you have a lot going on. Believe me, I get it. I'm in the same boat with my startup and feel completely underwater.

Oh trust me, I am well aware of all the things you have going on, she texts.

Now that's a loaded response. I can't let this one go.

Are you sure I didn't do something to upset you?

No.

Okay… so where is all this anger coming from?

Can you please leave me alone? I'm going to fail out of school if you keep bothering me.

Ouch. Bothering her?

I want to respond but I don't.

Instead, I pick up my econ text book and hurl it as hard as humanly possible at my closed door. It crashes against the wood with a thud.

It's not enough. My fingertips spark with rage and I grab the baseball bat leaning against my wall and decide my bookshelf is a perfect stand-in for Jaxon's face.

CHAPTER 27

Addison

WHY DID *I think majoring in biochemistry was a good idea?* I lament as I wash my hands.

I should have picked an easier major, or at least one where I can get more than four hours of sleep each night and not fail.

This semester isn't even half over. Brutal doesn't do it justice.

I have this sneaking suspicion I've forgotten to turn in homework or we might have a quiz today but I forgot to study.

Of course. I'm giving one hundred and ten percent, and it's still not enough.

There you are, princess, I hear a man's voice behind me.

What is Asher doing in here? I think. Turning around, I expect to see him. Except…

…oh god, I breathe.

"How did you get in here?" I stammer, tripping over my feet as I scramble backward.

He flips the knife in his hand. It catches the light from above and shimmers.

"Get out of here!" I cry as panic seizes my throat.

I try to scream but my body disobeys.

He's getting closer, *closer*, and I'm pressed against the wall now, trapped.

"*Please, please don't kill me,*" I beg, my voice barely audible.

He grins at me with decay-speckled teeth as he lunges for me.

I wake up.

———

You would think I was running from a bear by my ragged breathing. I'm sitting up in bed staring into the darkness of my bedroom. The only light is a scant hue coming from my laptop screensaver.

Fuck, the nightmares are back, is all I can manage to think. *Of course they are.* Now that I know the promise Asher made me was nothing more than a fucking lie.

I look at the clock on my phone. It's four a.m.

I went to sleep three hours ago.

If I take a sleeping pill now, I will undoubtedly miss my alarm. With midterms next week, I can't risk it.

I switch on my desk lamp and open my biology textbook. Might as well get a head start.

———

"You look like shit."

It's the first thing Ethan says to me when I open my dorm room door.

He's back for homecoming weekend. Lucky for me, he's decided his first order of business is to pay me a visit.

"I'm aware, Ethan," I say. He's right, and I'm too tired to argue.

"Seriously, Addison. Should I be concerned? You look worse than Mom."

I glare up at him. *Too far, Ethan.*

"Sorry, you know what I mean," he says.

I shake my head. "I'm tired, Ethan. This major is so hard and I'm so overwhelmed. I'm in over my head and…"

To my dismay, I start *crying.* No, not crying, *heaving.* I am bawling my eyes out like I'm a ruptured dam.

For once, Ethan is quiet.

Oh, I hate crying in front of Ethan.

"I'm sorry," I mutter, searching for a tissue I know I don't have and am forced to wipe my snot with my sleeve. *Gross.*

"Do you think it's possible you're putting too much pressure on yourself? You don't need to be in the top five percent of your class or whatever it is you said. You're going to drive yourself insane if you keep up this pace."

"Easy for you to say, Ethan. You barely have to lift a finger and you get the grades, get the amazing job you wanted, get the girl, get the…"

"Why did you say get the girl?" he interrupts, cutting me off.

"What?"

"You said get the girl. Addison, is there something you're not telling me about your love life? Is that why you're so sad?"

"What?! Ethan, no," I scoff. "Jesus, of all the things I said, *that's* what you hear?"

"And I'm not sad, Ethan," I argue. "I'm exhausted."

"Liar," he says.

"Ethan, I am not!"

"Whatever, well, I don't want to know about your love life anyway. The less I know, the better. Are you going out tonight?"

"*Am I going out?*"

The question is so absurd I almost topple over.

"No, Ethan! Did you not hear a word I said? I can't go out! I barely have enough time to take a shit!"

"GROSS, ADDISON! I don't need to think about you taking shits either!"

"Well, good to see your cheery disposition remains intact," he says with heavy sarcasm before telling me he's off to get white girl wasted.

I flip him a middle finger as soon as he shuts my door.

CHAPTER 28

Asher

"HEY, ASHER," a familiar voice calls from behind me. I turn around to…

"JESUS FUCK," I curse, spitting blood onto the floor after Ethan clocks me with a right hook to my fucking jaw. *"GODDAMMIT, ETHAN."*

"YOU FUCKED MY SISTER, YOU PIECE OF SHIT!" he screams, threatening to lunge at me again with another fist to my face.

Jaxon is a dead man.

"WHAT DID YOU DO TO HER, YOU ASSHOLE?"

Both Wyatt and Miles are restraining him while I try to pop my jaw back into place.

"Did you think you could do this and I wouldn't find out?" he spits as his saliva sprays everyone within a three-foot radius. He's stopped screaming at me, but his tone is just as deadly.

"I saw my sister today, and she's *fucking despondent.* I haven't seen her like this since her sophomore year of high school when that psychopath tried to sexually assault her."

My jaw's back into place now, and I need to get Ethan out of here before he causes more of a scene than he already has.

Homecoming weekend is crawling with alumni and the last thing we need is for sixty-year-olds to see two fraternity brothers beating the shit out of each other. Our frat's reputation on campus is on thin ice as it is.

"Ethan," I say sternly as the whites of his eyes flare at me. "Not here. Let's go upstairs."

He follows me, and I'm thankful to have Wyatt and Miles as a buffer between us. It's not that I don't think I could take him. It's that I *know* I could and I would probably do severe damage to that pretty face of his.

"Take a seat on your ugly ass throne," I say when we get to the common room of the suite I share with Wyatt and Miles. For whatever reason, Ethan loved to sit in this hideously upholstered armchair while he lived in the frat house and often referred to it as his throne. He would sit in it for hours when we had parties, holding court while Jaxon brought him trays of cocaine like a goddamned waiter. Every time I look at the chair, I see Ethan's smart-ass face, which is not ideal when you're fucking his sister. One day I'm going to throw that disgusting excuse for furniture out the window.

"You want a beer?" I ask.

"If you want me to throttle it at your head," he responds.

Okay, so it's like that, I see.

"Don't fucking lie to me, Asher," he says as I sit on the sofa across from him. "Did you do it?"

I pinch the bridge of my nose.

"Yes," I say. "I did."

The room fills with a silent rage before Ethan springs up again and starts whirling. I jump to my feet just as Wyatt and Miles grab either of his arms.

"I told you not to touch her, but you just couldn't keep it in your pants, could you?" he seethes.

Is he foaming at the mouth? Jesus.

"You could have any girl on this campus, but it had to be my sister."

"Ethan, I'm not some predator. We have a genuine connection, and I didn't do anything without her consent."

Okay, that one is a lie, but he doesn't need to know the details right now.

"Fuck you!" he spits in my face.

"Ethan, *I like her*!"

"Bullshit," Ethan sneers. "The only person you like Asher is *yourself*. You are the most selfish prick I've ever met!"

"Okay, yes! I'm a selfish prick! I'll admit it. But Ethan, please believe me when I say I've had feelings for her for a very long time."

"It's true," Wyatt says, backing me up. "He has."

Ethan looks at Wyatt like he's never been more betrayed.

"You knew?" Ethan snarls.

"Yes," Wyatt laments. "I knew, okay! I knew."

Ethan seems to have calmed down so Wyatt and Miles don't protest when he jerks his arms free.

"She looks really bad, Asher," Ethan says, his voice breaking with emotion.

"I think she's going through a hard time. Her major is truly that hard, Ethan," I say. "Most people drop out... or worse."

I don't need to add more color for Ethan to understand what *or worse* means.

He sighs.

"Listen, I don't want to get involved with whatever is going on between you two but just don't break her heart, Asher. We, my family, can't go backwards with her. You have no idea how bad it was a few years ago. The toll it took on our mom..."

Ethan shook his head.

"It was a very difficult time for our family."

"I know," I say. "I remember."

"Do not tell her you know about us," I say with a growl, although I'm not sure there is an *"us"* anymore. "She's under a lot of stress and you up her ass about this would only add to it."

"One last thing before we go back downstairs," I add. "Was it Jaxon who told you?"

"Obviously it was Jaxon," Ethan huffs.

That motherfucker is about to lose some fingernails.

————

I'm still bitter from Wyatt's refusal to let me pry off Jaxon's fingernails with my pair of pliers. A black eye and split lip were the compromise but definitely not as satisfying.

Punching Jaxon in the face, *twice,* did help my rage. But it didn't help ease my concerns about Addison.

Something is wrong. I know I did something, but I'm tired of guessing.

I won't interrupt your studying but can I please come and do a wellness check, I text.

I'm on my period, she responds.

Um, okay. That's a strange response, I think to myself.

Do you need me to pick up tampons for you? I ask.

No.

I rub my eyes with frustration. This girl is killing me.

Can I not see you when you're on your period? I text.

Wouldn't it be a waste of your time? she texts back.

What the fuck was that response?

That's it, I'm driving over there.

I stopped tracking her location at the beginning of the semester. It felt like an invasion of her privacy, even for me, but after she ghosted me for two weeks straight and then her brother punched me in the face, I turned my location tracking of her phone back on.

She forgets I'm an excellent hacker.

I'm halfway to her dorm when it occurs to me I should not show up empty-handed.

What do girls like when they're on their period?

Chocolate?

Flowers?

I detour to the local high-end grocery store before I check her location again to make sure she's still at her dorm.

I doubt I will be a welcome surprise but I hope the expensive chocolate bar and roses will help.

I knock softly. Light from inside peeks under the door so I know she's not asleep. I hear a rustling movement from within and then the door opens. The look of contempt on her face threatens to break me.

"What are you doing here?"

"I…"

Shit.

"I don't know. I needed to see proof of life and wanted to bring you these."

"Well, I'm alive. Happy?"

Barely. She looks barely alive and no, I am not happy.

"I'll leave," I say. I'm practically sulking.

She almost gets away with slamming the door in my face before I stop her.

"Wait," I say, pushing her door back open. "Take these, please."

Wow, she does not want to take them. I am failing miserably at this test.

"It's just chocolate and flowers, Addison. Throw them away if you want but please, take them."

She begrudgingly reaches for the flowers and chocolate in my hand, and our fingers touch.

My eyes plead with her to let me in.

"Goodbye," she says and this time, the door firmly shuts.

CHAPTER 29

Addison

"ADDISON, YOU CLEAN UP NICELY!" Anjali says, admiring her handiwork. She has spent the last hour doing my makeup to accompany the devil costume she's forced me to wear tonight.

"You are one sexy devil if I do say so myself."

I turn around to survey what she's dubbed a masterpiece.

"Damn, I do look good!" I say into the mirror. "Maybe I should rock a red lip more often."

"You could wear a potato sack and look good, Addison. But if a red lip helps you get your confidence back, I will come to your room each morning before class and do it for you."

I smile, taking another sip of my drink, careful not to let too much lipstick rub off on the cup. She's dragging me to this Halloween party at a random house off campus so she can meet up with a guy she likes. I'm trying desperately to be the supportive friend, but I'd rather crawl into a hole with scorpions than go out right now.

I haven't heard from or talked to Asher in almost a month. *A month.*

I had thought we were on the verge of dating until the

whole fucking ship imploded. I suppose I dodged a bullet. He probably would have either cheated on me or broken up with me in the end.

Still, I have this knot in my stomach.

Parties and nightlife are his turf, which I have intentionally avoided, so it seems reckless to venture out on Halloween when everyone and their mother will be out. Even though this school is huge, given my luck, I'm sure I'll run into him at some point.

The frustrating part is deep down I know I *want* to run into him. One, because I'm wearing this ridiculously hot and admittedly skimpy revenge costume, and two, because I miss him. I miss him badly.

And this is the part where I start to hate myself.

How can I miss someone who did something so vile to me? *How?* Who lied to me and betrayed me for who knows how long? He probably would still be seeing this girl behind my back if I hadn't gone to that party.

Or maybe I was the other woman, and he was seeing me behind *her* back.

Oh, that thought is just depressing.

I take another hearty gulp of my pre-game elixir.

"Anjali, this is very strong," I comment.

She gives me a wicked grin. "I know. But I figured you could use the liquid courage tonight since we'll likely run into that shit bag."

Right, Anjali hates Asher just as much as I do now.

I raise my drink. "To bringing shit bags to their fucking knees," I say.

Anjali squeals in delight as she clinks her plastic cup against mine.

"And then kicking them in the nuts!" she exclaims with glee.

———

We make it to the party on foot approximately twenty minutes and two mini-bottles of tequila later. I don't know who Anjali's alcohol hookup is but he or she came through big-time tonight. Once we arrive at the house party, I'm so tipsy that the shoving from all sides to get in the door doesn't even phase me.

In fact, I find it downright comical. All these idiots shoving their way into this dilapidated structure only to queue up for watery keg beer and an opportunity to flirt with someone.

The drunken spectacle surrounding us is a treasure trove of entertainment. The costumes are outrageous and for once, I'm enjoying the unsettling sway of the dance floor when Anjali grabs my hand and pulls me through a maze of hallways.

"Hi!" Anjali beams as she spies her current situationship, Anthony, who scoops her into his arms and twirls her around before setting her down.

Aww, cute.

"Let's get you ladies beers," Anthony says as we follow him to a row of kegs in the kitchen.

Anjali is making small talk with some of Anthony's friends as I stand beside her awkwardly.

"Can I have another beer?" I ask the guy manning the keg.

Anjali gives me a surprised look. "Okay, getting after it tonight! I'm glad to see fun Addison has returned!"

I don't have the heart to tell her this version of me is by no means "*fun Addison*" but it's a low bar.

Seconds later we're all blasted by the unexpected rise in volume of the music.

"Dance floor!" one of Anthony's friends howls. He follows that up by literally barking.

I am in the wrong place.

These are not my people.

I follow Anjali and company to the dance floor regardless. Thirty minutes in, and I really have to pee.

"Do you know where the bathroom is?" I scream in Anjali's ear.

"Down that hall, second door on the left," she screams back. *See, I had a suspicion she's been here before and it seems I am right.*

In pre-Anthony times, Anjali would have refused to separate. I have to pee, she goes with me. She has to pee, I go with her.

But she is in her Anthony era so I'm forced to go it alone.

Finally, I reach the bathroom and thank god the line is short *but the stench.* I'm pretty sure that's vomit in the wastebasket and piss all over the floor.

Ew.

I squat my behind over the toilet seat to relieve myself. Why are boys' houses always so disgusting? There is no point in washing my hands and I look over to see there's no soap anyway. No wonder everyone in college is always sick.

I push my way back to the dance floor, then panic.

Where is Anjali? I can't see her or Anthony, and Anthony is *tall.*

Shit.

Where are you, I text her.

I'm waiting on the edge of the dance floor, searching, when I feel my phone vibrate and I look down at the screen to figure out where the hell Anjali is when I realize…

…it's not Anjali.

It's Asher.

I wait, too scared to move. I have no idea where she is and I'm sure as shit not going to search for her.

Five minutes pass. Then ten.

Then I unlock my phone and feel a torrent of emotions come flooding back all at once.

Are you out? it says.

I do a mental scan of my current state.

Are you of sound mind?

No.

Are you emotionally ready to engage with him?

No.

Are you drunk enough to emotionally engage with him?

Maybe.

My brain tells me *maybe* is good enough so I keep going.

Are you drunk enough to physically engage with him?

Yes. No question.

We have a winner, folks.

Out at this house party on Berkeley Street, I respond. He immediately starts texting back.

The basketball house?

No idea. Anjali is hooking up with a guy who lives here.

Gross, get out of there.

Ha.

I'm serious, Addison, you shouldn't be there. It's not safe.

?

Meet me outside in 10, I'm coming to get you.

Scratch that, 5 minutes. I'm leaving now. I'm just down the street.

Oh.

Well, damn.

That escalated quickly.

I threw up in the bathroom, I text Anjali. I hate myself for lying to her. *I'm fine but need to go back to the dorm. Have fun! Love you.*

I push my way back through the crowd. I don't know this house, so it takes a while to orient myself and figure out the direction of the exit. I know I'm fucked when I catch my inner monologue praying I don't run into Anjali because she surely would insist on leaving with me.

Dammit. Getting out is harder than getting in. I'm nearly trampled as I push against the current of people to make my way outside. I take ten steps down the sidewalk when I see him standing tall as a statue, waiting for me.

"That took a while. I was starting to get worried," he says. It occurs to me I haven't heard his sultry voice in over a month.

"It's very crowded in there," I say.

"I can see that," he says, then abruptly pauses.

"What the fuck are you wearing?" he asks, eyeing me up and down with a look of displeasure.

Damn, I've even missed his possessiveness.

"I'm a devil."

He blinks as he takes me in, and I can't tell if I'm seeing a hint of admiration or pure scorn on his face.

"I mean, you look hot, but I don't like that you're practically wearing lingerie out in public."

"It's not lingerie," I protest.

"Addison, I could lick your tits right now if I wanted to. That's how exposed you are."

The thought of him licking any part of me reignites the tingle between my legs I was convinced had gone dormant over the last… month and a half? Wait, has it been that long since we…? I'm trying to do the quick math in my head.

"And what are you supposed to be?" I ask, trying to get the thought of him licking me out of my head. It looks like he's wearing his everyday clothing.

"Halloween's not my thing," he responds flatly.

Shocker. I'm not surprised by this man's disdain for forced holidays.

"Ever the rebel," I say with provocation, and we idly walk together down the sidewalk.

"Goddammit Addison, I want to cover you up. Can I give you my shirt?"

"No!" I hiss. "What, does it make you jealous that other people can see my ample cleavage?"

I added in the word *ample* for good measure even though it's probably a bit of an exaggeration.

His expression turns pensive.

"More than you'll ever know," he says quietly and my heart – *my stupid, weak heart* – betrays me.

"You say it like you care," I say. I know exactly what I'm doing with that statement – baiting him.

He scoffs, looking up toward the sky. "One day, Addison, you'll have to tell me what I did to make you think I don't."

He looks back down at me and stops walking.

"What are we doing here?" he asks.

"In general, or tonight?"

"Let's start with tonight."

"You tell me," I shrug. "You were the one who texted first."

"Come back with me?" he asks with such hope.

I hesitate, and a flicker of common sense enters my brain for just long enough to say *"this is a mistake"* before my best pal tequila shoves common sense aside and says without skipping a beat, *"fuck yes."*

"Okay," I breathe, committing to my decision.

What could possibly go wrong?

CHAPTER 30

Addison

DID *I want to prove something to myself? Was I lonely?*

I'm trying and failing to puzzle out an explanation for why I let myself come back with him to the scene of the crime.

He holds my hand as he leads me up the stairs. I can't help but think back to when I witnessed this exact scenario a month ago, except I was down below watching a different girl walking up these stairs, hand-in-hand with Asher.

I bite my tongue to stop myself from asking him whether he prefers blondes or brunettes. I suppose I'm neither and fall somewhere in between.

Dammit, inner monologue, shut up about my hair color and focus.

What are we trying to accomplish here?

Sex.

Okay, I'm more than certain sex is on the table. What else?

Revenge.

Not ready for that. What else ya got for me?

Kinky, rough sex.

My mind is an endless gutter of trash at this point, so I resolve to simply stop thinking.

How very brazen of you, Addison, is my last thought before crossing the threshold into the land of no return, otherwise known as his bedroom.

I notice multiple piles of books on the floor first.

"No bookshelf?" I ask.

"Had one but I beat the shit out of it with a baseball bat."

I cock my head to the side but decide I'm going to leave his response alone for now.

"Don't ask," he says.

"Wasn't planning on it."

Other than the messy piles of textbooks on the floor, his room in the fraternity reminds me of his bedroom back in LA except on a much smaller scale. Same four-monitor setup displaying stock market graphs and numbers, same style of desk chair and bedding, same smell of leather and tobacco.

Back in LA, he told me I was the first person he let inside his room, but now I'm wondering if that too was a lie.

Focus, I remind myself.

He drags a finger across my abdomen. "Are you wearing lingerie under the lingerie or is this it?"

I chuckle. "You're really triggered by my outfit, aren't you?"

"I'm triggered because I haven't seen you in over a month, and you're out parading your tits around for half of Harvard to see before I do."

"I didn't realize you had such a jealous streak."

"Me?" he asks incredulously, pointing to himself. "Have you forgotten who you're dealing with or are you just trying to get a rise out of me, princess?"

"Oh, I remember," I say with a devilish grin to match my costume.

A plan starts to form in my head, but he beats me to it, dropping to his knees to untie and remove my sneakers. I refuse to wear anything but comfortable shoes, even when going out.

I watch him with curiosity as he kneels before me and I start to feel how fast my heart is beating.

He wraps an arm behind my legs and pulls me in until his lips touch the front of my thighs. I feel the warm softness of them through the red fishnet tights I'm wearing. My eyes close instinctually, savoring the feeling of him as he plants slow, lingering kisses against my skin.

I hope he's planning to remove my teensy red pleather shorts next but he stands, eyeing me as he turns my body around and loosens the strings of the red corset I'm wearing.

It falls to the floor with a soft thud, exposing my breasts. He stoops down to pull off my shorts, carefully slipping them over one foot at a time so I don't lose my balance.

I'm now wearing nothing but a red lace thong and red fishnet tights.

"Oh my god," he snorts, stepping back to admire the full length of my disrobed body. "You have got to be kidding me."

"What?" I smile, but he just shakes his head.

He sinks down to his knees again and begins leaving a trail of kisses up my inner thigh until he can go no further. His lips only break contact with my skin for the seconds he needs to strip my fishnets off, then I feel his tongue kissing the crease where my thigh and groin meet.

My knees almost buckle as his tongue pushes my thong aside and slips between my folds. I catch myself on his shoulders, gasping as I feel his tongue burrow in further.

He pulls back, removing my underwear, and I watch him set my red lacy thong atop his desk.

"I'm keeping these," he says.

"I figured."

He crawls back to the edge of his bed and hoists himself upward, drinking in my nakedness. He drops my gaze, looking down into his lap. A strained noise gurgles up from his throat and his eyes, now damp with moisture, once again find mine.

"Addison," he breathes and the way he says my name, fraught with desperation and need, cracks the mask I've adorned tonight to conceal the wounds of his betrayal. I'm forced to look away, feeling the stinging sensation my eyes make right before I start to cry.

He pulls me toward him, and I climb onto his lap, kissing him in the same way I kissed him when I arrived at Harvard – ripe and so full of lust I was unable to contain myself.

I help him remove his shirt and unbutton the top of his jeans. I allow him to finish undressing himself, then guide him down until he's laying fully horizontal on the bed.

I snake my fingertips down his chest, landing on his now very erect penis and I find myself thinking I don't know why I've never realized how velvety soft his tip feels against my touch.

As I take him into my mouth, his eyes meet my coy gaze and I begin to caress his length with my tongue.

"Fuck, Addison," he groans, throwing his head back. His chest rises and falls with haste as I continue.

"Wait," he protests, reaching down. But I swat his hand away. I don't plan on stopping.

I know his rule but I don't want to relinquish my temporary power. He is writhing with pleasure, and I'm certain I have him right where I want him.

"Stop, STOP!" he shouts, sitting up, and I'm forced to let him go.

"Stop," he says again, panting. "You know the rules." And as if I'm nothing more than a bag of sand, he grips me under my armpits, pulling my entire body forward until my thighs are straddling his face.

The familiar hold of his fingertips digging into my outer thighs spreads me further apart as he starts to fuck me with his tongue, and I brace myself against the wall.

I feel him move upward to my clit now, sucking and swirling my sensitive spot until I'm moaning loudly against the back of my hand pressed in front of me. My thighs quiver violently as my climax comes roaring through me. I might actually drown him this time.

I love and hate how well he knows my body.

He guides me off him, and I look down to see his face glistening, slick with my cum.

"I need you," he breathes. "I need all of you."

"Then take me," I say, my voice barely above a whisper.

Please, I silently beg. *Break me.*

He reaches over to his nightstand to open the drawer for a condom, and I reposition myself in anticipation but then he throws me down on my back.

"I'm not letting you fuck me on top," he says as he parts my legs with his knees, working to angle himself at my entrance.

"Why?" I breathe in frustration.

"Because you come too quickly in that position, and I don't want to fuck you tonight."

I gasp as I feel him slide inside me, his girth spreading me apart as the familiar mix of pleasure and pain dance up my spine.

He whispers in my ear as he scoops his pelvis into my groin, gently and sensually thrusting himself inside me. "You can fuck me later, but right now, I'm going to make love to you until you release those tears you tried to hide from me earlier. Cry for me, baby girl, because I'm going to lick up every last drop."

———

"Addison, baby, let's go to the bathroom so you don't get a UTI," he whispers but I don't know if I can stand.

I don't know if I can even move.

I am a pulp of wobbly limbs and tender flesh as I try to pull myself from his bed. He helps me swing my feet over the side, and I can feel the solidness of the floor beneath my toes. But it does nothing to help my condition.

The fissure in my heart is raw and gushing blood, clawed open by the release of emotion Asher extracted when he made the outside world melt away and we were just two people joined together beneath the sheets, sharing one breath.

"Do you want me to carry you?"

"No, I can manage," I say, stretching to my feet.

He fishes out a T-shirt from his dresser, and I pull it over my head. The bottom hem skims my knees so it's hopefully enough coverage as we venture out into the common space.

I pull my shoes back on, because my bare feet are not touching the outside floor, and I follow him. I'm terrified when he opens his door to see who might be sitting on the clustered couches just past his bedroom. Lord knows they probably heard the show tonight.

Empty.

A small mercy.

He stands guard as I relieve myself, and then I wearily follow him back to our sanctuary.

"You've lost weight," he says when he pulls his T-shirt off me. "Why?"

"From stress, I think."

"How much?"

I curl into him under the covers.

"I don't know, maybe five to seven pounds."

"I don't like that," he says, kissing my forehead. "I would like you to put those five to seven pounds back on, please."

I close my eyes, content to indulge this fairytale of *us* for a few more hours.

CHAPTER 31

Addison

WHAT IS THAT GODFORSAKEN NOISE?

My head is pounding so badly I'm worried brain matter might burst through my skull. I roll over to see Asher clacking away at his keyboard, and each keystroke sends my blood pressure skyrocketing.

I pinch the gap between my eyes as I try to piece together the events of last night.

I texted Asher.

No, wait, he texted me.

We met up and came back here and judging by the soreness between my thighs, went at it for hours.

The truth has yet to be addressed.

And I'm violently hungover.

Fucking hell, tequila.

He must hear my stirring because he stops whatever nonsense he's typing.

"Morning, sunshine, how are you feeling?"

"Bad," I groan.

"Can you take me to the bathroom again?"

"Are you going to throw up?"

"Not yet."

He helps me put back on his shirt but insists I also wear his boxers, which are comically large on my small frame.

The reek of the bathroom this morning is unbearable, but I'm too hungover to care.

I am in bad shape.

"Can you please drive me back to the dorm?"

"Now?"

"Yes, I need to get home."

"But Addison..."

"I CANNOT express to you how urgent it is that I get home."

"Okay, okay, let's go," he grumbles, swiping his keys off his desk.

I don't know what his fucking problem is but I need him to check his attitude, immediately.

My humiliating walk of shame to his car does not help my mood. Loitering frat guys scurry out of our way as we walk past but not before giving me a lingering glance that makes my skin crawl.

I roll down the window as soon as we get in Asher's car, desperate for fresh air despite the chill.

My head is throbbing.

"When are we going to talk about what's going on between us?" he asks.

Fuck.

Never.

"Later," I say.

"Later as in six hours from now or six days or six months?" he says, his tone laced with bitterness.

Well, he's clearly also in a mood.

"Seriously, Addison, I need to know. Are you going to fucking ghost me again?"

"I didn't ghost you."

Oh god, I feel so sick.

"What would you call it then?"

"I told you, I'm really busy with schoolwork."

"You're full of shit."

I swallow down the bile clawing its way up my throat.

"Why are you pushing me away?" he continues. "If there's someone else, just tell me."

I shake my head as I look out the window. Thank god we're pulling into the parking lot in the rear of my dorm.

"Listen, I get your major is hard but I'm sick and tired of your bullshit, Addison. You won't answer my calls or texts. I can't find you for weeks at a time. I understand your major requires all your attention, but did you stop to think for one fucking second maybe I need you too? That my fucking dad died and I've been spiraling? Maybe for once, Addison, you could be a little less selfish."

Selfish. Did he just call me selfish?

"You're unbelievable," I seethe, and the hatred in the pit of my stomach roils.

"What did you say?" he taunts, like he wants to pick a fight.

I can't. I can't hold it down any longer.

"I SAID YOU'RE FUCKING UNBELIEVABLE, YOU LYING SACK OF SHIT!"

I scream at him so loudly I've stunned him into silence.

"You want to unpack that for me?" he says, his tone lethal, daring me to keep talking.

"You know what I want? I want to get the fuck out of your fucking car," I wail, frantically pulling at the door handle but it won't budge. He's locked me in.

"Please enlighten me, Addison. Why am I a lying sack of shit? What could I have possibly done to you other than put you on a fucking pedestal?"

"I KNOW, ASHER," I yell. "I know about you and her."

"Who?"

"The blonde one. But what do you mean, *who*? Are there

more? Am I just one of the many girls you like to fuck on rotation?"

He goes still, and I can see the muscles in his jaw clench.

"I saw you with her," I cry.

"When?"

"Why does it matter? I SAW YOU."

Fine, he wants the truth, I'll give him the fucking truth.

"Anjali and I went to a party at your frat at the beginning of the school year, and I saw you, Asher. I saw you make out with her and then follow her upstairs."

"Addison, I…"

"FUCK YOU! Fuck you, Asher! Do not say another fucking word to me. I am DONE with your lies."

I'm starting to lose my grip on reality.

"You LIED to me! You made me think you *cared* about me when you never cared. You just wanted to fuck me, and I'm the idiot who let you."

Every word out of my mouth becomes more and more hysterical as I scream.

"It was NEVER real, was it?"

"ADDISON, STOP FUCKING TALKING!" he yells, punching his steering wheel with his fist. His face has gone crimson.

"WHO IS SHE?" I scream.

"She's a girl I was hooking up with last year! She means nothing to me, Addison, please, you have to believe me."

"I believe NOTHING you have to say to me. Not anymore. And how DARE you call me selfish? You know what's selfish, Asher? How about *fucking me* without a condom? How about putting my health at risk when YOU KNEW you were seeing other people!"

A vile, horrible intrusive thought bursts into my mind, and before I can stop myself, I say it.

"You deserve to spiral, Asher, and I'm sorry you never got

to know your dead dad because it sounds like you two cheating pieces of shit would have had a lot in common."

Shaking. He is shaking.

I've never seen rage like I see now on Asher's face. I can see his blood boiling and I'm certain if he could breathe fire, he would have burned me to ashes by now.

I brace myself for what he's about to say next but I only hear the click of the doors unlocking.

"Get. Out."

CHAPTER 32

Asher

I DON'T KNOW where I'm headed or why. I just know I'm driving.

A shrill ring has been in my ears for the last fifteen minutes, and I can hear nothing other than this sound.

Someone is going to die today.

I'm vaguely aware I've returned to my frat by the jostling I feel when I pull into the gravel parking lot behind our house.

The back door of our frat is outlandishly heavy, but it floats like a feather when I fling it open. I curl my fingers into fists and roll my neck as bodies scramble out of my line of sight like cockroaches. By the time I make it to the common room of my suite, I can see nothing in my peripheral vision other than red. There could be a three-headed lizard singing nursery rhymes on the wall for all I know.

Someone says my name; I think it's Miles. But I blow past him into my room and slam my door so hard, the wood cracks.

And then I see all her shit still scattered around my room: the red corset, her red fishnet tights, her lacey red thong. My room, my sheets, my FUCKING HANDS, still smell like her, and I'm going to lose my...

"Asher, are you okay?" Miles asks, opening my door.

Mistake.

I look at him like I'm going to rip out his throat and then I see that *fucking chair.*

I don't know if I pushed Miles out of the way or simply smashed into him, but once I lock eyes on Ethan's ugly fucking throne chair, I ROAR.

Glass shatters everywhere.

I am screaming so loud I feel veins popping in my neck. Then I drop to my knees as everything goes black.

———

"Is he alive?"

I blink my eyelids open to see Wyatt vigorously shaking me.

I'm on the floor, but why?

"Jesus Christ, he's alive," Wyatt says, sounding relieved.

"The fuck's going on?" I rasp, surprised by how hoarse my throat feels.

"You threw Ethan's throne out the fucking window, that's what happened," Wyatt tells me.

My eyes close again as I try to remember.

Addison.

Addison happened.

"Be careful, there's glass everywhere," Wyatt says as I sit up.

Miles is gingerly scooting large shards over to the wall with the tips of his sneakers.

"I did this?" I ask.

"You stormed in here about twenty minutes ago looking like you just ripped an eight-ball of cocaine," Miles explains. "Your veins were popping out of your neck and honestly you looked like you were possessed by a demon from the ninth circle of hell."

"Broke your door," Miles continues, pointing at my bedroom door, now cracked straight down the middle. "I made the mistake of trying to see if you were okay and I thought you were going to snap my neck. Thank god you decided to throw Ethan's chair out the window instead of me."

"Did I hurt anybody?"

"I mean, that's to be determined," Miles says. "We don't know where you were or what you did before this all happened."

"You hurt the fucking chair," Wyatt says. "It broke into a thousand pieces when it hit the ground. You do realize we are three floors up, right?"

"So it's dead?"

"*The chair?*" Wyatt asks. "Yeah buddy, I'd say the chair is dead."

"Oh yes, it's beyond repair," Miles confirms, looking out the window.

"Do you know how much this is going to cost you?" Wyatt wails.

"Wyatt, I do not give a fuck."

"Rich asshole," he mutters under his breath.

"What the hell happened?" Poor Miles sounds exasperated.

"I fucked up," I say.

"CLEARLY," Wyatt chides.

"Who was here last night?" Miles asks.

"Addison," I confirm wearily.

"See, I told you," Miles smiles to Wyatt. "Pay up."

"You assholes placed bets on my downfall?"

"Old habits die hard," Wyatt shrugs.

"So, did you two get in a fight or something?" Miles asks.

It's all coming back to me now – last night, the drive this morning, every damn thing she screamed at me, how I threw her out of my car.

"She knows about Chloe," I admit.

"You told her?" Wyatt asks in disbelief.

I shake my head.

"Worse. She was here the night it happened. She saw us kissing on the stairs."

Wyatt and Miles are both looking at me like they've seen a ghost.

"And you had no idea?" Wyatt stammers.

"No. But I sure as shit do now. I was driving her home this morning and, because I truly am a piece of shit asshole, decided to pick a fight with her about ghosting me. Then she snapped."

"Everything came out," I continue. "Everything."

I start laughing at how much pain I feel – as if one thousand knives are bearing down into my chest at the same time, slicing a gaping hole through my middle. I deserve this. I deserve to be nothing more than carrion for the crows.

"She hates me," I say, shaking my head. "Hates. Me."

And then I do something I've never done before.

I sob.

CHAPTER 33

Addison

THE ROAR of Asher's G-Wagen tears through the parking lot, and I hear his tires squeal in objection at the turn he's no doubt taking far too fast.

I start running but I'm not quick enough.

Vomit sprays from my mouth and onto the concrete in front of me. I heave again, doubling over.

Not so brazen now, are you, Addison?

———

Pounding. It's so loud it sounds like it's coming from the foot of my bed.

"ADDISON, OPEN THE FUCKING DOOR!"

My eyelids snap open.

Oh god, I'm in another nightmare. Connor's here… and he's… he's breaking into my room.

"If you don't open the FUCKING DOOR in the next ten seconds I'm going to break it down!"

My breath quickens as I try to make sense of my surroundings.

A thundering slam smashes against my door, and I jump

to my feet. I hear another male voice outside my room say, "That's enough! She's asleep!"

I'm clutching my shirt, cowering against the windowsill debating if I should jump to freedom as another blow to my door rattles the entire room like an earthquake.

"I don't give a FUCK, WYATT!" I hear.

It registers then it's Asher, and he will literally break down my door if I don't stop him.

"What the fuck is wrong with you?" I hiss, throwing my door open. "Are you out of your mind?"

I don't know this man standing in front of me. This is not Asher. This man is haggard, his face is sickly pale, his eyes are rimmed with purple and red splotches, a dusting of blood covers his knuckles, and he's glaring at me with eyes so hollow, I'm not sure this person in front of me is human.

"Yes, he's very much out of his mind," Wyatt answers for Asher, and I shoot him a scornful look that says *"how dare you bring Asher here in this condition?"*

I also didn't realize Wyatt knew about us, but that's the least of my concerns now.

"Let me in," Asher growls, now mere inches away from me.

If I say no, he'll force his way in anyway and he's already made such a disturbance, I'm worried one of my neighbors has called campus security.

I open my door to placate him, and he pushes past me.

"Are you going to be okay?" Wyatt asks me.

"LEAVE, WYATT," Asher shouts from within.

"I'll be fine," I say but I'm not convinced.

I shut my door and turn to face the beast now perched on the edge of my bed. I've never in my life seen him, or anyone for that matter, at this level of angry. I swallow my nerves and muster every ounce of courage I have to walk the four steps it takes to stand across from him. I can feel his rage filling every inch of space around me, sucking all the air from the room, and I'm terrified.

I hope he's not expecting me to be the first to speak because I don't think I could find my voice even if I had to scream.

He draws in a breath and my throat tightens.

"I am sorry, Addison, for my part in what happened between us," he says in a deadly voice. I imagine it's how a madman might sound right before he snaps. "But you need to own the part you played as well."

I open my mouth to tell him to go to hell, but he cuts me off.

"Because I fucking needed you."

I pause, blinking my eyes wide, not sure I heard him correctly.

His tone has gone ice cold and he's shaking with rage. My core turns leaden.

"I FUCKING NEEDED YOU!" he screams, and I jump back. I'm so startled that I've practically scrambled on top of my desk to create more space for the volume of his voice.

"I NEEDED YOU," he screams again, banging his fist against his chest and even in the dim light of my room, I see veins bulging from his neck and his nostrils flare. Tears take shape in his eyes, now crazed and glassy with rage.

"I NEEDED YOU, AND YOU WEREN'T THERE!"

Oh god, I think I'm going to vomit again.

"You left me," he snarls through clenched teeth.

"You were my only tether to life, Addison, and you ABANDONED ME. I've spent every waking hour since you left me wishing I was FUCKING DEAD, and the only reason I'm not, the only reason I'm still walking this earth, is because I made a promise to you. When you gave me the greatest gift I've ever received in my life, I promised you I would keep you safe and I will never, as long as I'm capable of breathing, break that promise."

Despite how scared I am of Asher, I can't help my spite.

"What was the gift I gave you – *my virginity*?"

He huffs an angry laugh.

I meet his glowering stare and let him study me. Seeing him this broken takes every bit of courage within me not to drop to my knees and beg him to forgive me for what I said. It was despicable. But my virginity was not a gift for him to throw back in my face as his reason for making that promise because *that promise* to keep me safe is what made me come to Harvard this year, *that promise* made me leave my sick mother behind, *that promise* made me think his feelings went beyond a simple hookup. I was content to believe it was just sex, but *that promise* made me think he cared.

He blinks, eyes darting away from mine, and when they return, the look of unbridled fury has been replaced with something that looks a lot like… despair.

I take in his softened countenance, trying to decipher what caused his abrupt change in emotion. His pleading eyes lock with mine, and I feel as if I'm truly seeing him for the first time tonight – not the screaming maniac who tried to break down my door out of anger but the broken, desperate boy who had no other choice.

I see unrelenting pain. I see a deep hurt that looks like it's been there his entire life and that he keeps hidden with his wrath and arrogance.

"No, Addison," he says, his gravelly voice heavy with grief. "The gift you gave me was not your virginity. It was hope."

"Hope?" I question.

He looks up at me with pain-drenched eyes. "I was spiraling," he croaks. "My biological dad died, and it felt like my purpose for living died with him. Growing up, I told myself *one day* I would become somebody – somebody so successful and powerful, he would drop to his knees with regret. But he took away my chance at vengeance. He left me. Again."

"I had given up. I tried to drink myself to death. Some nights, I was so drunk and high, I wasn't sure I would wake up the next morning. A part of me didn't want to. But you had happened. It was so new, and I still wasn't sure how you felt about me. But when you told me you weren't coming to Harvard this year, I panicked. I needed you here."

My throat has gone dry as sandpaper, and I try to force down a swallow.

"That day I spent with you in LA, Addison. Those twenty-four hours – they saved me. *You* saved me. I promised you I would keep you safe and I knew then I couldn't give up. You were counting on me. That knowledge alone was enough to keep going."

The fury in the air is gone, and I feel nothing for him but sorrow. He had tried to show me his wounds before, but I was too callous, *too busy*, too concerned about my own needs to grasp he had cried out to me in hopelessness. But I had only turned him away.

I feel wetness trailing down my cheeks before I realize I'm crying. I go to him, taking his face in my palms so those green-hazel eyes of his are forced to meet me.

"I am so sorry," I rasp, and my resolve, my hatred, the need I felt this morning to make this man bleed, breaks.

He cups his hands around mine.

"I will never forgive myself for hurting you, Addison," he whispers. "I deserved everything you said to me today."

"No, you didn't," I breathe.

"Yes, Addison," he says, refusing to tear his eyes from mine. "I did. I'm a contemptable human being who treated you horribly. I was selfish and I'm ashamed of myself. I'm ashamed of what I did. I was so excited for this semester and I've done nothing but fuck it up. Honestly, I don't know what's wrong with me. It was just…"

"Shitty and stupid," I finish for him.

"It was shitty and stupid and I'm the one who is so, so sorry."

I close my eyes and kiss him, tasting the whiskey on his tongue.

"You've been drinking."

"Since nine this morning after you left."

"Jesus," I whisper. I don't even want to know what other substances are floating in his system. We can deal with the question of where this leaves us tomorrow.

"Please don't leave me," I plead. "Please. Stay."

"For you princess, I'll never leave," he whispers.

CHAPTER 34

Asher

I'VE BEEN awake for thirty minutes, listening to the sound of her soft breathing as I feel her ribcage rise and fall under the arm I have wrapped around her. The bed in her dorm room is far too small for both of us to fit comfortably, but I like to think she would still sleep curled into me even if the bed were three times this size.

I'm both terrified and elated at what I've done: elated because I think I've gotten her back but also terrified for the exact same reason.

It's the second of November, and in about sixty days from now, I board a plane to London. I'm supposed to spend a pivotal six months there with a world-renowned professor who can apparently make or break my career, and ultimately my success, as a startup founder.

Between the drama and shortcomings of my personal life this semester, I'm concerningly behind. At the beginning of this school year, I had already missed critical milestones, but I rationalized my delays as a gap I'd surely be able to close in September and October.

But I failed. *Badly.*

You would think Addison ignoring me for nearly two

months straight would have given me time and space to work, but the only progress I managed to accomplish was more self-loathing and draining every bottle of whiskey in sight. Every morning, there's a knot of anger gnawing at my insides. But there's no cure for whatever hateful disease festers inside my mind. *Or at least I haven't found one yet.*

There's only alcohol and drugs and numbness, and I don't know if I'll ever find myself again.

I hate that this is the only version of myself Addison has seen.

If only we could have started our journey together twelve months after we did. I wish we could hit pause and start anew next summer: after Oxford, after I got my mind and shit together, after I was well on my way to becoming a success. I would be the man she deserves at that point, not a shell of myself like I am now.

Life doesn't work out the way you wish.

What terrifies me the most is I think I love her.

No, *I know* I love her.

I am in love with her and I cannot stop myself from obsessing about her.

Where is she? Who is she with? Is she with another guy? Is she thinking about me? Does she need me? Should I find her? How can I make her love me back?

I *cannot* stop, and it's a problem.

I don't realize I've been fitfully tapping my thumb against my chest when she stirs, stretching her body against mine as she wakes.

Her eyes blink open, and I wonder if she's replaying all I said to her last night in the same way I did when I woke up. There's still plenty that's been left unanswered.

She closes her eyes again, and I take it to mean she's not ready to have this conversation, which is fine because I need to get up and take a piss anyway.

"Any requests for autographs this time?" she asks when I

return. Apparently, my presence on this floor has become quite infamous.

"Seven but I politely declined," I jest.

I crawl on top of her and kiss my way down her neck to the collar of her T-shirt. I must have passed out before her last night because I usually don't allow her to sleep next to me wearing clothing. Sleeping with her skin against mine has become a craving, and I struggle to fall asleep unless my hand can feel the curve of her hips, my chest can feel the graze of her teardrop-shaped breasts, and my thighs can feel the slick arousal she often has when she's dreaming.

"Oof, my bladder," she protests and scrambles out from under me.

I follow her to the bathroom, scanning each stall and shower before allowing her to proceed. I stand guard outside and wonder why the sound of her urinating gives me goosebumps.

We snuggle together in bed, neither of us saying a word. I suppose it's my responsibility to have this conversation.

"Can we talk about last night?" I ask.

"Which part?" she responds.

"Which part do you want to start with?" I say, which I know is a cowardly approach.

"Wyatt knows about us?"

I wince, knowing she has outwitted me, as this is by far the easiest part of last night to discuss.

"He does, yes."

"And who else?"

I know where this is headed.

I run my free hand through my hair. "A lot of people."

"Is my brother one of those people?"

Shit.

"Yes."

She goes quiet, contemplating this news.

"He hasn't said anything to me," she says after a while.

"I told him not to," I say.

"Why?"

"Because you have enough on your plate already. You don't need his bullshit added to the mix."

"Wow," she says quietly. "I'm truly surprised he didn't say anything to me. Normally he loves to reprimand me for my choices."

"Yeah, well, that shit's not going to fly with me," I say.

"Did you threaten him?"

"I didn't have to. He knows better."

"Why did you do it?" she asks. "With Chloe?"

Now for a hard one.

"Honestly, I don't know. Maybe because I was drunk and high and angry and lonely… and hopeless."

"So you slept with her?"

"No, not the night you saw us. I did not sleep with her."

"But you…"

"Please don't make me tell you." I cringe at the thought of telling Addison what I did with Chloe that night. But if she asks, I won't lie to her.

"When is the last time you slept with her?"

"Last semester – in the spring."

"Not over the summer?"

"No, not since you came into the picture, if that's what you're asking."

"Did you go down on her?"

Interesting.

"No."

"You aren't lying?"

"I swear on that promise I made you, I'm not lying."

She's gone quiet, and I'm assuming she's working through what I *did* do with Chloe now that two possibilities have been eliminated.

"Addison, it meant nothing to me. You have to believe me."

"How am I supposed to trust you?"

It was the right question to ask. And I didn't know how to answer.

"Will you give me a second chance?"

She turns pensive, and I don't like that I can't see her face.

"Come here," I say, pulling her upward to rearrange our bodies so she's seated in my lap and I can look directly into her eyes.

"Will you please give me a second chance?" I ask again.

"I think we have different priorities," she says.

"What is that supposed to mean?"

"I'm never going to be the girl who gets drunk at frat parties Tuesday through Saturday. I came here to accomplish a very specific purpose, and if something were to happen to my mom while I'm here, squandering away my opportunity, I would never forgive myself."

"I know you are not this girl," I say. "I don't want you to be."

"Then why don't you respect my boundaries when I say I need to study?"

"Why don't you let me crawl into bed next to you when you're done studying?"

I knew it was a deflection and not an answer, but I feel like there's something she's not saying.

"Because I'm tired," she says.

Now I'm confused.

"And?" I ask.

"And I can't fuck you every night, Asher."

"Hold on," I say and I can feel my brows furrow at the accusation. "You think the only reason I want to see you is so I can fuck you?"

She drops my gaze. "Is it not?" she says, quietly now.

I am flabbergasted. I hardly know how to respond.

I lift her chin back to face me so I can search her eyes for a semblance of understanding. *How could she possibly think sex is all I want from her?*

"Addison." I breathe out her name. "Make no mistake, I love having sex with you. I love worshipping every inch of your body. But a physical relationship is not all I want from you. It's not enough for me. I want to crawl in bed next to you so I can hold you in my arms and feel your heartbeat. I want to see your eyes light up when you talk about whatever frog you were dissecting in class that day. I want to see the dimple you have on the right side of your mouth appear when you laugh at my bad jokes. I want to *know you*, Addison. *All of you.*"

She's biting her bottom lip, and I want to tell her more of how I feel but I don't. I'm not ready.

"*Please*," I beg.

"What do you want from me, Asher?" she asks.

It's a loaded question. I draw in a breath, exhaling loudly and thinking carefully before I answer.

"One more chance. And to sleep next to you most nights, even if it's not every night. And for you to return my texts in a handful of hours so I know you're okay."

"That's it. That's all I want," I swallow, and I mean it.

She stills, and my pulse skyrockets.

It feels like the rest of my life hinges on whatever she says next.

"Okay," she says, exhaling a long sigh. "Just one more."

CHAPTER 35

Addison

"YOU DID WHAT?"

Anjali is basically shouting at me across the ridiculously small space of my dorm room.

"Addison," Anjali wails. "I thought we agreed you would never get back together with that fuckboy! Can't you see he's playing you? That he's telling you whatever he thinks you need to hear to win? This is a game for him, Addison!"

I pinch my eyes closed. Part of me knows she might be right, but the other part of me desperately wants her to be wrong. How could he have said what he said and not meant it? Is he that skilled of a liar?

"I don't want to see you get hurt, Addison, and I know guys like Asher. I've *dated* guys like Asher. They are pieces of shit. They never change even when they say they will. They'll lie through their teeth without hesitation, directly to your face."

"But what if he's not?" I say meekly. "What if he's actually one of the good ones and just had a bad night, like he said?"

"HAVE YOU BEEN BRAINWASHED?" she yells. "Addison, do you hear yourself making excuses for this guy *already*?"

I did, and she was right.

"Ugh, great, so, now what?" she asks, annoyed. "Are you going to be spending every waking moment with him? Will I never see you again? I'm going to have to join a sorority now to make a new friend since you're ditching me for a guy."

"No! Absolutely not. And I'm not ditching you for a guy," I say firmly. "If he doesn't respect my boundaries with school, he's done. I get it, I'm a fool. I don't know why I agreed to give him another chance. I just felt so... bad for him. He was so compromised and raw, and his emotions were bleeding out all over the floor and I couldn't help myself. I was weak – *am* weak," I correct myself.

"Are you in love with him?"

"Oh my god, no! I barely know him."

She studies me with suspicion. "I think you are."

"I'm not!" I insist.

"I think you are but don't want to admit it to yourself."

I shake my head in disagreement.

"Well," she says in what I can tell will be her last stand. "Lord help you if you are, because if you love a boy like that, you've got a long road of pain ahead of you."

CHAPTER 36

Addison

"ARE you sure you don't want me to come with you?" Asher asks as he pulls up to the airport. "I can book a flight and be there tonight."

"No, it's fine," I say, "Besides, I don't think Ethan is ready to see us together."

Truthfully, I was dreading the inevitable conversation I know Ethan would force me to have about Asher.

"I'll miss you," Asher says as he pulls me into his arms. I kiss him for as long as I dare before I'm sure airport security will scold us for lingering.

"I'll miss you too," I say, and god do I mean it.

I haven't been apart from Asher for three weeks. Well, that's not entirely true. There were a few days off here and there. But how am I supposed to say no when he wants to pick me up from the library at three a.m., then drive me back to my dorm so I can nestle beside him in bed and sleep like a baby? It's like my subconscious brain remembers I've gone to bed with my dark angel gladiator at my side so nightmares of Connor remain at bay.

Asher is headed to New York for Thanksgiving. His

stepdad has family in Connecticut, so they usually spend the holiday there.

"Promise you'll tell me if Ethan crosses the line," Asher says again as he pulls his lips from mine. I already promised him I would but I reassure him. "I will, I promise."

He gives me one last lingering kiss on the mouth, followed by another on my cheek, then neck. I hear him breathe in the smell of my hair before he pries himself away. I see the same longing look in his eyes as I saw when he dropped me off at LAX months ago. This time, though, three words dangle between us. I turn to head into the airport, and he turns to get back into his car. Neither of us say them.

Did he want to? Does he feel as deeply about me as I do about him?

I'll never know. At least not now, and I wish I knew why the absence of those three unsaid words has me crying in the airport bathroom.

––––––

Ethan has been surprisingly quiet since returning on Wednesday night. I was certain the first words out of his mouth would be, *"Why the fuck are you sleeping with my friend?"* Maybe it was all a show for my mother, who looked frail but not terrible. I've definitely seen her look worse.

I love cooking Thanksgiving dinner with my mother. In healthier times, we would go shopping together, stopping at all sorts of specialty stores and farmers' markets to find just the right mustards and jams for the charcuterie board, the perfect vegetables to roast alongside the turkey, and the most decadent wine to accompany the meal. I'm underage, but ever since I was old enough to drive, she's let me have a few sips from her glass. It was our little secret.

This year, she sends my dad and I out with a list, but it wasn't the same without her. My dad cannot cook to save his life, so I volunteered to do all the prep work of chopping and dicing and marinating.

Ethan didn't grace us with his presence until late Wednesday night, flying in from San Francisco on possibly the last flight departing that day. He said work was extremely busy and perhaps that was true, but I wondered if he was purposely avoiding me.

It's so unlike Ethan to hold back his feelings, and I'm sure he has plenty about Asher and I. I don't know what they talked about, but I don't doubt for a second Asher had threatened him. My guess is whatever rage Ethan has been bottling up since their encounter is at severe risk of boiling over, hence the less time at home, the better.

Ethan and I are cleaning up the dishes together now, listening to music and awkwardly not speaking. He had been very reserved in his wine consumption at dinner, but a wayward glance in his direction tells me he's diligently righting that wrong.

"Pretty good wine, huh?" I ask.

He scoffs.

"Sure, Addison. You a wine connoisseur now? Did Asher teach you that?"

Oh, here we go.

I put down the dish sponge and turn to look at him.

"Just say it already, Ethan."

"Say what?"

"You've been biting your tongue all evening. Don't think I didn't see the look on your face when Mom asked me if I had any male suitors. Say whatever you want to say to me so we can get this over with."

He laughs a bemused laugh into his wine glass as he takes a notably large gulp. "You don't have the stomach for what I want to say to you."

I fling the filthy sponge at his face, and it collides with a wet plop across his nose.

"Ethan, I am eighteen, nearly nineteen, years old and I have been letting you berate me with your endless bullshit since the Connor thing happened, and I am done."

He goes stiff at the mention of Connor.

"What? You didn't think I would go there? Let's fucking go there, brother. Let's get it alllll out." I draw out the word *all* until it sufficiently covers what has now been almost four years of his shit. "Say what you want to say. The floor is yours."

He refuses, and his disengagement makes me furious.

"You want to call me a slut? You want to tell me how stupid I am for getting involved with Asher? That I'm reckless because I spread my legs for a guy three years older than me? That I deserve whatever pain happens to me when he breaks my heart because we both know guys like him don't end up with girls like me?" I provoke.

"Huh?! Is that what you want to say? Now's your chance, Ethan, to tell me. *I'm asking for it.*"

He levels an irritated and somewhat shocked glare at me before draining the rest of his wine glass. He snatches up the bottle and grabs a second glass from the dish rack.

"Sit down," he says, walking to the now cleared dining table. "We need to have a chat."

He pours me a glass of wine, which makes me even more nervous. Despite the copious amounts of underage drinking he did, he's always had a double standard when it comes to me.

"First of all," he begins, "I'd like to start with the fact that I'm not an idiot and I've known you've both had a crush on each other for a long time. It just thankfully took you both a while to figure it out."

"Secondly, let's not forget I lived with Asher for two years in our frat house. He is by no means the worst, but he is far from the best, and if I had to pick the right guy for you, Addison, I can't say I would pick Asher. Obviously, I'm good friends with the guy so he has his redeeming qualities. But from what I've witnessed firsthand, he is exceptionally self-ish, manipulative, and cold. He rarely does things out of kindness unless he has something to gain. Also, like the rest of my fraternity, we all party far too much, and he's no excep-tion. He's angry and pensive, and I've never seen him be particularly sweet to women. He can be ruthlessly vicious if you piss him off. I don't think he understands consequences. It's not a matter of *if* he will break your heart, it's when, and it's not because guys like him don't fall for girls like you. You two are actually perfect for each other if I'm being honest. I just don't trust him not to fuck it up."

I take in a long breath and an equally long sip of wine.

Jesus.

"That's… um…" I shake my head at the diatribe about Asher's shortcomings. "That's a lot to take in, Ethan."

"Listen, I said this to Asher when I confronted him at homecoming, and I'll say this to you. I'm not getting involved in whatever is going on between you two. I just don't want to see my baby sister get hurt. I'm worried about you, Addison. I always worry about you."

"I know, Ethan," I say, thinking it was the sincerest thing he's ever said to me.

"And I know I don't know a damn thing about life," I continue. "But you have to let me try, Ethan, and figure it out myself, even if it means I get hurt."

"We can't go back, Addison," he says. "*I* can't go back. I can't go back to that time. It was horrific seeing you so destroyed. You could barely function. You couldn't get out of bed for weeks. Months went by, and I was genuinely worried that I would get a phone call from Mom that you didn't make it. I don't think my heart can endure seeing you in so much pain again, Addison. It broke me."

"Maybe that's why I'm so hard on you," he says, wiping tears from his eyes.

"Ethan," I say, taking his hand. "What happened with Connor was awful. Living with the memory of a mentally unstable stalker trying to sexually assault you at knifepoint has not been easy. When something like that happens to you, it's not something you ever forget. Every day, I look at this scar on my jaw and remember it. But I was a sophomore in high school when it happened, Ethan, and I *survived*. If I can survive that, I can survive Asher screwing me over. I'm more resilient than you give me credit for."

He nods, and I feel a massive weight lift off my chest. After all these years, it feels like we finally have reached an understanding.

"What are you two going to do next semester when he's abroad?" Ethan asks, clearing his throat.

"I don't know," I admit. "We haven't gotten that far."

"Are you boyfriend and girlfriend?"

I'm embarrassed to admit we haven't had that conversation either. I don't know if I'm his girlfriend or just a girl he's hooking up with.

I shake my head. "We haven't talked about it yet."

Thankfully, Ethan doesn't have a clever retort. If he does, he doesn't say it out loud. It still stings. Isn't three weeks in a college relationship equivalent to three years in the real world? Shouldn't we have established by now what we mean to each other?

"Enough about Asher. How are your friends?"

Nonexistent.

"I have one good friend named Anjali. She's in my major. We met the first day and just clicked. There are a few other girls in my classes I'm friendly with, but honestly it's hard to make friends when you're in the library twenty-four-seven."

"You should join a sorority," Ethan says.

"Anjali says that too. I think she'll try to join one next semester. It's not really my thing though, Ethan – the whole forced friends thing."

"So classes are hard?"

"Classes are brutal."

"You think you'll stick it out in this major?"

"Ethan," I huff. He already knows my answer.

"I know, I know," he says, smiling as he sips the rest of his wine. "Become a world-renowned researcher, find a cure for cancer, save mom, the whole hero thing, I know."

CHAPTER 37

Asher

IT'S quiet in the econ building today. I've been looking forward to this.

At last, I've made considerable progress on my startup over the past few weeks. Addison keeps a tight schedule – rising with the sun and holing up in the library until I force her to leave at two a.m. to get some sleep. She's exhausted, but the semester's almost over.

I've adopted her working hours, which means I'm not partying until four a.m. most nights. Instead, I'm sleeping in bed next to her. This also has considerably improved my Chloe problem because it's been easy to outright ignore her, shirking the direct conversation I know I should have. I'd rather sweep it under the rug for now, and she seems to have gotten the message anyways. I haven't gotten a ranting, drunk text from her in over two weeks.

Thanks to Addison's absolute refusal to do anything but study all day and night, my schedule has emptied these last few weeks, making space for a much-needed surge in productivity. The only problem is I can't get the damn girl out of my head.

When I'm not with her, I'm thinking about her. I'm

daydreaming about our future. I'm making a list of all the places I want to take her when next semester is over. Hell, I'm practically mapping out our road trip through Europe next summer, even though I haven't told her of my plans yet. I'm smiling at the thought of playing tour guide around Oxford when she comes to visit me on spring break. I've saved an online shopping cart of erotic toys I plan to send her next semester for her to use during our phone sex sessions, which, if up to me, would be nightly.

Sleeping next to her and not being allowed to ravish her each night is killing me, but it was the deal I made to get her back. I can only suffer through a few nights of celibacy before I'm nearly bursting for her. She knows this and even if she's weary, she'll let me take her because we both know she needs the release just as much as I do, if not more.

I don't know how I'm going to make it through next semester. I'll probably end up having to fly her out every other weekend for my own peace of mind. I'm not even slightly worried about myself, but I worry if I don't keep her satiated enough, she'll seek her pleasure elsewhere. Besides, phone sex and my hand will suffice for my temporary fix, but they're no replacement for the soft, pink flesh of her pussy.

Goddamn, her body is a drug.

For her, I turn feral. No one else has ever come remotely close.

The connection we have when I'm inside her is euphoric. It's more than sex or a physical joining. It's an emotional interlocking of souls, and I never want us to stop.

A shudder runs down my spine at the thought of her beautiful, perfect body intertwined with mine. She's probably landed in LA by now, and I wonder if Ethan is already back home as well. I hope he's not being a dick to her about our relationship, for her sake and his. I can't have him stressing her out while she's home. I need her to eat, to put back on the weight she lost over the last few months, and that won't happen if Ethan is being his usual charming self. I should have gone with her.

I don't think Ethan will be outright hostile to her but I wouldn't put it past him to say a few choice words about my past behavior. I certainly was no saint during my first few years of college and unluckily for me, he was right by my side during most of it. I wouldn't say I was a womanizer but I don't think I gave off the impression I'm a relationship guy.

How could I have predicted what would unfold between Addison and me? Until she kissed me in her pantry, I didn't believe I had a shot. I was convinced I would spend the rest of my life vying for her attention, stuck admiring her from a distance. But when she kissed me, our spark was undeniable, and a tiny seed implanted inside me. A festering, buzzy feeling replaced the apathy and disdain I had felt toward my life. I've come to recognize that buzz as hope.

After being with her, that seed grew inside me. I had purpose. I had a reason. I had *her*.

"Asher!"

Professor Friedman's voice snaps me from my reverie.

"Professor," I say as if I hadn't just been lost in thought about Addison for the better part of an hour.

"I'm glad to see you here," he says. "And admittedly, surprised."

"Surprised?" I ask.

"Well, yes, after your notable absence from this office over the past semester, I was worried you may have had a change of heart."

"Oh, absolutely not," I assure him.

"Well, what happened then? Something in your personal life?"

"You could say that," I respond, not wanting to delve into the drama of my spiral and dead dad.

"Is your family in good health?" he asks.

"Perfectly fine, thankfully," I lie.

"Well then perhaps my suspicions are correct. Is it a girl who has you so distracted?"

I clear my throat, not appreciating the remorse he's making me feel about Addison.

"I did meet someone, yes."

"Is it serious?"

"It's too soon to tell," I say, wondering if I'll regret my lack of honesty.

"I see. So typical college romance then. Intense, yet fleeting."

Out of respect, I wasn't going to argue with him. But by no means did I intend for my relationship with Addison to be fleeting.

"Have your pilot trials started yet?"

"They have," I beam, grateful for the change in subject.

"When can we look at the data?"

"I'll have thirty days of data by next week," I say.

He frowns. "I was hoping for more. You should have at least sixty days of data collected by now. When did the trials start?"

"Three weeks ago."

"Hmm," he hums. "That's disappointing."

It's been a long time since someone has made me feel this small, and I loathe nothing more than the feeling of inadequacy.

"You know, Asher, when you're at Oxford, Professor Rossario will demand you eat, sleep, and breathe your startup. There can be no room for error, distraction, or daydreaming. He will sniff out any lack of devotion in a heartbeat, no matter how you try to hide it. Make no mistake, he'll have no issue throwing you out of his mentorship program. And not only will he throw you out, but I fear he might speak negatively about your dedication and potential to startup accelerators and venture capital firms. I've seen him be vindictive before when he felt someone was wasting his time. I don't want that to be you, Asher."

"Remember, it's not only your reputation on the line here, but mine as well. If I don't think you're ready for the kind of rigor Professor Rossario requires, I'll suggest he proactively decline your participation next semester."

I swallow at his threat.

"The stakes are high, Asher, and based on what we've discussed previously and what I've seen from you so far, this semester aside, you're more than ready and capable. I'm betting on you, Asher, and I hope you rise to the challenge."

"I will," I croak.

He gives me a satisfied smile. "Let's connect after Thanksgiving. I'd like to review the data you have and work on your narrative. We can discuss how to package your initial findings into an investor presentation, which will likely be the first deliverable Professor Rossario will ask for when you meet him at the top of next year."

"Of course," I say. "I'll put a meeting on your calendar for next week."

He pivots but turns back around.

"I'm also looking forward to seeing who you choose."

"Who I choose?" I ask, perplexed.

"Yes," he says with a wry smile. "Whether you choose the girl *or yourself.*"

CHAPTER 38

Addison

CAN *you come to my room?* I text Anjali.

We had planned to be at the library hours ago so we're already behind.

We are so close to being done with this semester. One last final exam stands in the way of our freedom: Biology 101. This is where dreams are shattered and the top five percent is made. One exam is worth half the grade.

You fuck up, you fail, and all the sleepless nights and countless hours spent in the library would be in vain.

I can't afford to fail. Getting invited to participate in the summer fellowship program is my nonnegotiable.

The final exam is seven hours long.

Seven.

You have to be escorted to and from the restroom. You're not allowed to eat, and only water is permitted.

It's pure torture, but pain is nothing for a masochist like me.

Pain is where I thrive.

Nothing is going to derail me.

But damn, this small cardboard box in my hand is sure trying.

I hear noisy footsteps down the hall and the jostle of a backpack. I'm nearly certain it's Anjali so I swing open my door before she can knock.

"What's up?" she huffs, and I can tell she's annoyed by this detour.

"Shut the door," I say.

"Okay," she says, on edge. "Is something wrong?"

I hold up the box.

"Fuuuuuck," she draws out.

"Fuck, Addison," and I can see the panic across her face. "Have you taken it yet?"

I shake my head. "I've been too scared."

"How do you take these things anyway?" she asks, grabbing the box. "It says you're supposed to pee on it right when you wake up for the most accurate reading."

She looks at me. "It's nine a.m. You'll have to wait until tomorrow."

"I can't," I say, my breath quickening. "I haven't peed yet and I need to get this over with. I need to know *now*."

"YOU HAVEN'T PEED YET? Aren't you dying?"

"I was waiting for you," I admit.

Oh god, I'm so fucked.

"What are you waiting for?! Take it already! Do you want me to go in with you?"

I nod.

"Okay," she sighs. "Let's go."

I'm on the floor of my dorm room with my head in Anjali's lap trying not to hyperventilate.

I hadn't realized my period was late until yesterday when Anjali asked if I had tampons in my backpack.

"Maybe it's stress," Anjali says. "You've been extremely stressed, Addison, you even said so yourself. Didn't you say you lost like five pounds?"

"It was fifteen actually. I weighed myself when I went home for Thanksgiving."

"Fifteen?" Anjali says in shock. "Addison, you were already tiny. You don't have fifteen pounds to lose. Between the stress and weight loss, not getting your period on time is completely explainable."

I'm picking nervously at my cuticles as I examine the ceiling.

"How late did you say you are?"

"I'm almost three weeks late, Anjali."

She curses under her breath.

"Do you and Asher not use protection?"

"We do," I say. "And I have an IUD."

"Oh, then there's no way you're pregnant."

I withhold telling her about the time we didn't. Although the last few months have been a blur, I'm terrified the timeline aligns.

"Okay, it's time," she says. "Do you want me to do the honors?"

"Yes," I breathe, my voice is shaking. My whole body is shaking.

What would I do? Keep it? Get an abortion? I wouldn't even be able to do that until I got back to California. I'd have to tell Asher. Oh god, this is the worst possible thing that could happen right now. How am I going to focus on studying if I'm fucking pregnant?

"Congratulations," Anjali says, and my eyes widen. I'm certain I'm going to vomit.

"You're not pregnant."

———

Anjali left hours ago.

I told Asher not to come get me tonight because I'd planned to be here until the wee hours studying for tomorrow's final. Or I guess today's: about six hours from now.

Fuck.

It's 2:30 a.m., and the light drizzle of snow from earlier has turned into a fucking blizzard. I'm not walking back to the dorms in this, so I guess I'm sleeping here tonight.

"Fuck me," I say aloud, shaking my head as I look out the double glass doors. The angry swirls of wind and snow are a ghastly sight. "I should have left when I had the chance."

"Probably would have been smart."

I whirl to see him nonchalantly leaning on the wall behind me.

"When did you get here?" I stammer.

"Ten minutes ago. Call me crazy but I had a hunch you would still be here. Seems like I was right."

His taunting smirk makes me want to melt into a puddle at his feet. Despite the fact I think it's totally inappropriate to exhibit public displays of affection in a library, I pull his face into mine and kiss him.

I really fucking kiss him.

"Thank you," I swoon. I can't seem to let him go.

"What would you do without me, princess?"

"Sleep on the floor of the library," I answer matter-of-factly.

"Well, we can't have that, can we? he says. "Let's go get your stuff and get you home. Big day tomorrow."

"Don't remind me," I exhale with trepidation.

"You'll be fine," he says. "I guarantee you no one has worked as hard as you have this semester."

He might be right, but I still feel woefully unprepared.

"Holy shit," I exclaim, gasping as the icy wind steals my breath. I've never been more grateful to see Asher's hunter green G-Wagen in my life.

"This storm is not fucking around," Asher says as he climbs into his car. He's already made sure I'm tucked safely inside.

He truly does treat me like a princess.

I'm forcing him to sleep at his frat tonight. I need the space so I can focus. This is it – I'm ten meters away from the finish line, and I can't afford to take my foot off the gas. Still, I don't object to door-to-door service.

"Remind me of your plans after your exam tomorrow?" he asks.

"Going to dinner with Anjali and a few friends from my major, then out to a house party she wants to attend. She's hell-bent on rushing a sorority and said some sophomores from one of the sorority houses invited her. I'm going for moral support."

"That's kind of you," he says, although I perceive a hint of disapproval. "I won't see her before we leave for New York, which means I won't see her until the beginning of next semester." I don't know why I feel the need to explain myself.

"It's fine," he says in a way that doesn't make it sound fine. "I'm supposed to go out with the guys tomorrow anyway. It's the last night for us too before we all go our separate ways next semester."

Right, Asher going abroad. How could I forget?

"Why don't you text me when you get to the house party and then I'll come get you – say around midnight?" he says. "We can leave whenever we want the following morning because your flight isn't until ten p.m., and it's only a four-hour drive to New York from here."

Grinning over at me, he says, "Maybe I'll still be able to convince you to push your flight out a day."

Asher really wants me to stay the night with him at his stepdad's condo in the city, and I have to say I'm tempted. He's staying in New York for the holidays, then flying to Switzerland with his mom and stepdad to ski for a week before making his way to Oxford.

I'm trying and failing not to think about the fact I have less than forty-eight hours left with Asher. God knows when I'll see him again. We've talked about me flying out to visit him, but who knows how soon it will happen? He'll need time to settle in at Oxford before he's ready to host a visitor.

I shake the thought from my head. I've been in denial about his semester abroad for the last few months. It arrived much faster than I anticipated.

I'm sure we can figure out long distance, but I don't think it will be easy on either of us. Over the last eight weeks, we've formed quite the co-dependent relationship.

I push down these feelings of impending dread. We've made it back to my room, and I've still got one critical mission ahead of me before I can indulge all my worries and anxiety about next year.

"Thank you," I whisper, stretching up on my tiptoes to kiss him, and it takes every bit of effort from both of us to pry ourselves away.

"Good luck," he says, giving me one final kiss on my cheek. I savor it but I want more. I've denied him sex for the last five days while I've been in final exam hell. And god, I hope he pulls out all the stops tomorrow night because I want him to fold me like a lawn chair.

I want him to break me.

CHAPTER 39

Addison

I AM RUNNING, screaming, crying with glee.

"WE'RE DONE!" Anjali shouts, jumping into my arms so forcefully, we nearly tumble to the ground.

"I never thought this day would come," I wail into her shoulder. Tears of joy run down my face.

I entered the auditorium riddled with fear and left a free woman. It's over. What's done is done.

"We are going to get SO drunk tonight!" Anjali exclaims. "Should we start now?"

"Hell no!" I protest. "I got like two hours of sleep last night. I need to take a nap."

"Oh shit, I forgot I left you at the library. Did you sleep there?"

"No, Asher came to get me."

Anjali rolls her eyes.

"I know, I know, you still don't like him," I say.

"At least you're not pregnant with his *baby*," Anjali says much too loudly, and I cringe.

"Anjali, SHUT UP!" I yell.

"Can you imagine little Asher babies running around trying to unalive ants with a magnifying glass in the summer?" she cackles with laughter. "Because you know he did that kind of evil shit as a kid."

"Oh my god, Anjali," I huff. I guess I deserve her jeering since I made her an accomplice in my overly dramatic pregnancy scare.

"You go take a nap," she instructs me. "I'm going to pack for my flight tomorrow morning and we'll meet up at seven p.m. to head to dinner?"

"Perfect," I confirm, thinking I haven't felt this level of happiness and relief in ages.

———

"My clothes are too loose, but my cheekbones look fucking snatched," I say to Ethan on the phone, admiring myself in the mirror. It's been a long while since I dressed up to look desirable.

"I'm not sure that's the right way to think about things," he says. "But congrats regardless on surviving your first semester in the most difficult major at Harvard. When do you find out if you made the five percent thing for the fellowship program?"

"They post our final standings online forty-eight hours after the exam, so I guess I'll find out when I'm back in LA."

I still haven't decided if I'm going to stay the extra night with Asher. Frankly, I could have taken a flight to LA from Boston but he convinced me to book a flight from JFK. I'm sure he was secretly hoping the drive to New York would lead to me switching my flight, especially since he said he'd pay for the change fee and the upgrade to business class if I did.

I really want to get home though. I desperately miss my mom.

"You're coming home for the holidays, right?" I ask.

"Of course! Someone needs to force-feed you."

"Ethan! For the millionth time, I'm not trying to lose weight. I've just been very, very stressed. Jesus, you and Asher both."

I instantly regret the slip.

"What did you say?" Ethan asks and I know he heard me.

"Nothing," I say quickly.

"Is your *boyfriend* joining us for the holidays too?" Ethan says snidely.

"He's not…," but I stop myself.

He's not what? My boyfriend? Am I really about to say he's not my boyfriend? After everything this semester, have we really failed to talk about the status of our relationship?

A wave of concern crests over me. *He must think of me as his girlfriend*, I rationalize to myself, *especially the way we've talked about me coming to visit him in England.*

"He's going to be in Europe with his parents," I say to Ethan, composing myself. "Sorry to disappoint you."

There's an audible scoff on the other end of the phone.

"Okay, well, enjoy your night off," he says.

I start to hang up when he cuts in and says, "Addison…"

"What, Ethan?" I ask, anticipating another cautionary tale about Asher.

"I'm serious. Go celebrate tonight. Enjoy yourself. You've earned it."

CHAPTER 40

Addison

THE BITTER FLAVOR of beer mixed with cheap sake has never tasted so good.

I force down the last gulp of my sake bomb as glasses clank against the table.

"How absurd was that last essay question?" Lily belts out, wiping a trickle of beer from her chin.

"Literally, I thought I was going to collapse," Anjali jokes. "I think I spent an hour on that question and I don't even know if I actually answered it correctly."

"Who do you think will be in the top five?" Lily asks our small study group of four, now out to celebrate our victory.

"Definitely Marcus and Sajid." Yvonne says. "Addison, you definitely will be top five."

"I hope we all get top five," I say, pouring myself the last bit of sake.

"If I make top five, it will be a miracle," Anjali says as I roll my eyes. I know the grades she's gotten.

"Ladies, I should get going," Lily says, looking at her phone. "My flight is at five a.m. tomorrow, which means I basically have to get up in four hours."

"Or you could just stay up all night!" Anjali jests.

"Maybe you can pull that off, Anjali, but not me," Lily says as she stands and puts on her coat.

"I'm going to head back to the dorms too," Yvonne says. "I'm exhausted. Have fun tonight, you two, and have a great break!"

We exchange hugs, and I scurry off with Anjali in the freezing winter snow toward this house party.

"So who are we trying to impress here tonight?" I ask as my teeth chatter.

"Ugh, Addison. It's ironic how much you despise the Greek system, yet you're dating one of the most notorious frat boys on campus."

"We're not dating," I correct her.

"Of course you're dating!" she exclaims. "You've been sharing the same bed for the last month and a half! You're practically married at this point."

I want to disagree but it's so damn cold outside, I don't want to expel energy speaking.

"Still don't know what you see in him," Anjali continues.

"I don't know," I huff as my warm breath crystalizes in the icy air. "He's like heroin. I can't stop."

I'm a bit stunned at my own honesty. *Is this how I really feel?*

"Spoken like a true addict," Anjali says. "Let me remind you, heroin kills people. Oh! This is the house."

Finally. I share my location with Asher as we walk inside.

Thankfully, this party is far less crowded than the last one I attended with Anjali. That memory of Halloween night still feels rancid on my tongue.

I don't recognize anyone here, which causes an instant wave of anxiety. This house, like the one from Halloween, is disgusting. Pizza boxes, beer cans, and who knows what else are scattered everywhere. I'm pretty sure if I allow my eyes to linger, I'll see more than a few cockroaches.

People actually sleep here? I shiver as I think about lying in bed with a cockroach darting across the blankets.

"Oh! Let's play beer pong, Addison!"

Anjali seems excited, but this idea could not be more dreadful to me.

"Anjali, I'm awful at this game," I say, hoping to convince her to pick a less public form of humiliation.

"Stop! It'll be fun!"

"Noah!" Anjali calls as she drags me across the room. "We want next game!"

A boyishly cute face is deep in concentration as he studies his shot and aims the ping pong ball at the rack of cups across the table. He throws, sinking the ball with a plunk.

Strange. He looks oddly familiar.

"Anjali, do we know him?" I ask, nodding toward Noah.

"He was in our bio class but dropped out," she confirms.

"Ah. Right. I thought he looked familiar."

There was no forgetting that ear-to-ear smile and dirty-blonde hair. It was wavy, but he kept it neatly styled in a way that made me want to tousle it with my fingers.

Noah and his partner won their game easily, and I knew they would make short work of Anjali and me.

"Anjali, I don't think you understand how bad I am. We're going to lose in like three rounds."

"Fine," she rolls her eyes at me. "Noah! Come here."

She beckons him over with a curve of her finger, and I wish I had a shred of her confidence.

"Noah, you remember Addison, right, from biology?"

"Of course, although I doubt she remembers me," he grins. I've never heard him speak but I'm struck by how perfectly his voice matches his appearance – boyish, playful, and full of himself.

"Why would you say that?" I ask with extra sass.

"Because you would always sit in the front row. I just

figured since I always sat near the back, you never bothered to notice me."

A flirt. Dangerous.

"Well, anyway," Anjali presses on. "She's really terrible at beer pong, so instead of girls versus boys, how about you play with Addison and I'll play with Jack?"

Wait, does she know everyone here? How did she find the time to meet all these people?

"Deal," Noah says with a devilish smirk.

We rack our cups as the boys fill them with beer, and the game is underway.

"Why did you drop out?" I ask Noah as I try to aim my ping pong ball. I throw but miss wildly. This is embarrassing.

"Sorry," I cringe. "I told you I was bad."

He laughs. "You're cute."

I blush and realize it's been a while since someone has openly flirted with me.

"Dropped out because it was fucking awful and I don't want to be a doctor," Noah answers. "But I take it you and Anjali stuck through it?"

"We did," I confirm. "Had our final exam today."

"How was it?"

"Brutal, of course. It was seven hours."

He whistles. "Damn, seven hours?! Absolutely not. Thank you for confirming my earlier decision to run far, far away from pre-med."

"Yeah, but I don't want to be a doctor either," I say.

"Why are you doing this then?"

"I'm a biochem major. I want to be a researcher – either cancer or vaccine development."

"That's very noble of you."

I think he means this as a compliment, but it feels strangely belittling.

"You're Asher's girlfriend, right?" he asks, tossing a ball across the table.

I go rigid. This is an odd pivot in conversation.

"Um, I guess," I respond.

"You guess?" he asks incredulously.

"He threw a chair out our frat window because of you so I'd think that means you're more than friends."

"*A chair?*" I ask in disbelief.

He raises his eyebrows and nods in confirmation. "Yep. I'm curious what a nice girl like you is doing with a psycho like him."

I'm a bit shocked at his brashness. "Sounds like Asher has quite the reputation," I say. "You said you're in his frat?"

"I am," Noah says. "I pledged this semester."

"Wow, you're really bad!" Noah teases as I miss another toss. Anjali is up next, and she lands her shot.

How is she so good at this game?

"I'm giving you all of these to drink," Noah says, scooting every cup Anjali and Jack have landed over to my side of the table. "Better start chugging."

I give him an eye roll but I start guzzling. The thing about watery keg beer, I've observed, is it starts to taste not so terrible after the second or third. And dare I say, this game is actually becoming *enjoyable*.

We're down to the last cup when Anjali's partner deals a final blow.

"Want to play the next game with me?" Noah asks.

"No, she does not," a grizzly male voice cuts in from behind.

A quick glance between Asher and Noah tells me all I need to know about their feelings toward one another. Noah could not look more uncomfortable, and Asher looks like he's going to kill him.

"When did you get here?" I ask, trying to keep the mood lighthearted.

"Five minutes ago. I texted you. Did you not see it?"

I think he's legitimately angry.

"Oh sorry, I was playing."

"So I saw," Asher says with a sneer. "Ready?"

"Yep, let me just say bye to Anjali."

I walk over to my ride-or-die and give her the biggest hug I can manage.

"No!" she frowns. "Has your prince come to fetch you and take you away from me?"

I give her a puppy-dog frown.

"I'm going to miss you over break," I say. "I'll call you."

"You better," she says. "Call me as soon as the final standings are posted, even if it's bad news for me. I'll still be happy for you."

"Sort of," she teases.

"Oh, shut up, Anjali, we both have an equally good shot at getting in the top five percent, and you know it."

"Ugh, okay, fine, BYE," she huffs as she hugs me one last time.

CHAPTER 41

Asher

THAT LITTLE BITCH Noah knew exactly what he was doing.

When I walked in and saw Addison standing next to him playing beer pong with a stack of empty plastic cups in front of her, I wanted to flatline him then and there.

I hate that fucking snake.

I told Wyatt not to let him pledge our fraternity, but we let his ass in anyway. Apparently he's a double legacy, and his daddy wrote us a sizeable donation at the start of the semester.

More like a fucking bribe.

I decided not to say anything to Addison about him because she looked like she was genuinely having a fun night, and I didn't want to rain on her celebration parade. That is, until we were in the Uber on the way home and she said, "Noah told me you threw a chair out the window?"

Dead man.

"Did he?" I play it off as nonchalantly as possible, mostly because I'd prefer not to revisit that day for numerous reasons.

"What else did pretty boy Noah tell you?"

She laughs. "You don't like him."

It's a statement, not a question.

"Do you?" I ask. Now I'm just being petty.

"What?" she laughs, cocking her head back. "I only met him tonight!"

"Remind me why we're talking about him?" I ask. I'd rather talk about throwing the chair out the window than hear his name on her lips one more time.

"The chair ... you did that?" she asks.

"Right. The chair. I did do that, yes."

"Why?" she's still laughing when she asks.

"Because I was sick of looking at it," I reply.

"So not because of me?"

I can tell by the way she's looking at me, she secretly likes the idea of me hurling a piece of furniture out a window because of her.

I gaze over, and she's giving me a giddy smile.

"Fine," I concede. "Of course it was because of you."

"Wow!" she cackles and my heart swells to hear such earnest laughter escape her lips, even if it's at my expense. I don't know how much longer I'll get to hear her laugh and I want to soak up every second of it.

"We have some things to talk about," I say as she wipes tears of laughter from the corners of her eyes.

"Oh, yeah, I know," she says. "Do we have to talk about it tonight?"

"No," I say. But I do plan to confront her about the pregnancy test I found in her wastebasket as I was decorating her room earlier, although I'm inclined to wait until after I fuck her. I can feel my temper getting the best of me and I don't want it to spoil her fun.

The thought of her keeping something so monumental from me, even if the test results were negative, has me irrationally angry. In fact, our entire situation has me irrationally angry. Seeing her flirt with Noah tonight didn't help my already strained disposition.

I want to chalk it up to her lack of social life this past semester, but I'm also not a fool. Dickheads like Noah will move in on her like piranhas the second I board my plane. Wyatt and Miles will be here to keep tabs on her, but it's not her I don't trust. It's everyone else. Still, a little reminder tonight wouldn't hurt.

I had thought about letting her choose – whether she wants me to be the guy who licks her tears while making love to her or the guy who fucks her until she's born again. But I decide instead of giving her what she wants, I'm going to give her what she needs.

"It can wait until tomorrow," I say, "We do have a four-hour drive to New York ahead of us."

CHAPTER 42

Addison

"OH MY GOD," I gasp as I open the door. I turn to look at Asher in disbelief. "You did this?"

"The fact that you asked if I did this makes me a little concerned, princess," he says with a sly grin on his lips. "Would there be someone else who would sneak into your room while you're out celebrating and decorate it with balloons and champagne?"

I grab him by his jacket collar and back us both into my room as I greedily kiss his mouth.

"I forgot you have such a jealous side to you," I say, baiting him.

"You haven't seen the half of it," he growls. "And if you think I won't punish you for that flirtatious stunt you pulled tonight with your new little friend, you're sorely mistaken."

"I wasn't flirting!" I insist. Truthfully, though, I might have been just a little.

"Liar," he says.

"I wasn't…," I whimper.

"Lie to me again," he whispers, biting my bottom lip as he pinches my left nipple so hard, it takes my breath away.

"I'm not."

He squeezes harder and my voice catches in my throat at the pain.

"Do you know what happens when you lie to me, Addison?"

My fear turns me on much more than it should.

"Undress yourself," he commands.

He perches on the edge of my bed as he likes to do, taking me in with his arms crossed as I stand before him, stripping down to my lacy bra and panties.

"All of it," he says in a way that makes me tremble.

I pull my panties off first and then unhook my bra, tossing it to the floor. He gives a low grunt of approval.

"Now spin around like a good girl."

I begin to spin for him like one of those dolls in a music box.

"Slower."

The lack of speed somehow makes me dizzier. I finally turn a full circle, locking in on his face as he studies me like a starving lion. I swallow, wondering what acts of depravity are coming next.

"Where's the toy I got you?" he asks. The dark, twisted tone of his voice makes me think he's going to chain me to the bed.

"In the bottom drawer of my desk."

"Get it."

I fetch the toy but notice as I lean over, my hands are shaking.

"Sit on your desk."

Any other night, my desk would have been littered with papers and textbooks but now that exams are over, it's barren.

I do as I'm told.

"Spread your legs," he says.

I feel strangely self-conscious but I lift one thigh at a time to spread them outward.

"Wider," he growls.

I scoot them a little further.

He levels a disapproving glare at me and stands, closing the distance between us until he's hovering directly over me.

"I said," he snarls, seizing my right ankle.

"WIDE…," he jerks my right foot upward and smacks it on the corner of my desk. I wince at the painful grip he has on my ankle as he holds me in place.

"…ER," he finishes, as he does the same to my left foot. He places it on the opposite corner, which forces me to hinge backward and balance on my tailbone.

My opening is angled up at him, and my breath turns erratic because I know what's next.

"Pleasure yourself," he demands as he moves my hand holding the vibrator between my legs. "Show me you know how."

I give him an unsure look, but the quiver in his jaw tells me he's not backing down.

Have I used this thing before?

Yes.

Am I an expert at it?

Absolutely not.

I press the button and hold it against my clit, willing my body to relax. I'm nervous if I don't show him I can climax on my own, his version of doing it for me may not be so gentle.

I close my eyes and allow myself to moan into the vibrating suction. Not a minute passes by before my breath begins to hitch and a fiery need builds inside my core. *Bless the efficiency of machine-powered intimacy.* I can feel my own slickness against my fingers and remember why I liked this toy so much the first time I used it.

I open my eyes to see him looking down, watching me. He watches the vibrator pulse and suck against my clit while studying the position of my hand and fingers.

I don't know why seeing such concern on his face, such

desire to make sure I have a mastery of my own body, turns me on even further.

The temperature of the room feels like it climbed ten degrees higher, and I feel beads of sweat running down the small of my back. I'm panting like a ragged dog, and I'm maybe thirty seconds away from climax when he drops to his knees.

His tongue spears into me, and I fucking explode, shaking violently with release.

I'm still holding the vibrator against me when he rips it out of my hand and throws it on the floor, his tongue still lapping inside me. I hear the thud and wonder for a split second if it's broken.

But I don't have time to worry because in the next second, he stands and snatches me off the desk by my waist, dropping my feet to the floor. The skin around my sides burns from the friction of his hands but I don't have time to think about that either before he grabs the hair at the back of my head and pulls hard.

"Get on your knees baby girl and beg for this dick," he growls.

I do. I don't hesitate. I want him, need him, inside me. I need his pressure. *I need it badly.*

I claw at the button and zipper of his jeans to take them off because apparently my version of begging for him involves putting his cock in my mouth.

"Fuck, Addison," he groans as I caress his length with my tongue, nibbling playfully at the velvety skin of his tip. I removed his boxer briefs when his jeans came off, which gave my mouth undisrupted access to his testicles. He had already been halfway to peak extension, but I have him swollen and fully erect in seconds.

"Up, UP!" he barks, and I do as he tells me.

He hoists me up to the edge of my bed, balancing me again on my tailbone, and rams himself inside me. The pain from his fingertips buried into the flesh of my hips as he slams me up and down on himself is almost as overwhelming as the pressure of his girth threatening to tear me in half.

It hurts so badly, but I'm screaming for more, and I fucking love it.

I bounce like a rag doll on him, and our groins slap together so wildly, it sounds like a wet towel on skin.

"Destroy me," I beg him and I'll be dammed if he didn't rise to the occasion.

CHAPTER 43

Asher

"DESTROY ME," she pleads like a woman dying to meet her maker. Those two words shred apart the only remaining tether I have to my restraint.

I wrap an arm around her waist and am distantly aware of how hard her back slams against the wall when I move us to a position where I have more leverage. I need the solid wall behind her so I can drive into her further. The edge of the bed just wasn't cutting it, but fuck, the wall isn't either.

I can see her second release building as her nipples tighten, but I don't appreciate how she has yet to scream my name. *Not so fast*, I think. I plan to make her earn it.

I rip my body from hers and practically toss her on the bed. She crawls backward and I'm delighted to see she thinks I'm going to allow her to finish while she lies on her back.

Far from it, princess.

My only regret for the night will be missing the stunned look on her face when I flip her over onto her stomach in one quick motion. I grab hold of her hips and pop her ass up but stop myself from taking her like a glutton. I want to memorize the look of her glistening, pink pussy, dripping with desire and the release she already had, before I thrust my cock deep inside her.

"Scream my name like a good girl," I grunt as she moans, begging me for more. I pound inside her, harder and harder and harder, until she gives me exactly what I want, exactly what I need to hear – my name on her fucking lips. She screams my name, and not a moment too soon. I burst alongside her, convulsing as my orgasm unleashes itself, blasting my cum into her pussy like water from a fire hydrant.

———

As I pull out, I see my cum run down her inner thigh. She's panting into the pillow, arms folded by her ears like she might launch herself into a yoga pose.

I turn her over to see her face. Concern strikes me that perhaps I had given her more than she bargained for.

"Are you okay?" I ask, my voice barely a whisper.

She nods, eyes closed, and I can see she's not.

"What's wrong, baby?" I plead. I'm lying next to her, half on top of her thanks to this miniscule-sized bed, watching what I think is a civil war unfold in her head.

She blinks her eyes open.

"You didn't use a condom again," she whispers.

"I thought we were past that," I say. And earnestly, I did. We had talked about it, I had taken a full STD panel test, there were thankfully none, and I figured we were ready for this.

"I'm not past that," she answers.

"Is this because you thought you were pregnant or is there another reason?" I ask, and she looks at me in shock. "What? Did you think I wouldn't see it in your wastebasket?"

Tears roll down the sides of her cheeks.

"Why didn't you tell me?" I ask, trying my best to remove all hints of aggression from my tone.

"Because it was negative."

"No, why didn't you tell me *before* you took it? Did you not think I would want to be there for the results? It's a pretty big fucking moment, Addison."

"It's not a big deal," she says. "I just didn't think…"

"No, you didn't think," I say, cutting her off. "And for the record, I consider any matters concerning my sperm inside you to be a very big deal. Don't pull any shit like that with me again. The next time you need to take a pregnancy test, I want to be holding it under you while you fucking piss on it, understood?"

"I'm sorry," she nods.

My words had come out more hostile than I intended, and each passing second of silence is a painful reminder of just how fucked our situation is – and how fucked I am. I'm furious with myself.

"What would I have done?" she asks as her voice cracks.

"I think you mean what would *we* have done?" I correct her. "And the answer is *we* would have done whatever *you* wanted to do because it's *your* body. But if you're asking what I think about the idea of having a baby with you, I would say yes in a heartbeat. Are you kidding me? I would be over-joyed. There's no other person on the planet who I'd want as the mother of my children. But if you weren't ready, we would discuss our options and try again in the future."

She breathes out a long, shaky sigh. Maybe my response surprised her, but it was honest.

Utterly fucked.

"Speaking of taking a piss," I say in a poor attempt to change the subject, "you do not want to be sitting on a six-hour flight with a UTI."

She groans, and I don't blame her. She's already taken up her post-coital sleeping position, curled into my side just where I like her. The magnitude of this moment is not lost on me, and I'm terrified at the possibility this could be the last time I get to hold her like this. Something tells me she knows this as well. But she's doing an equally good job hiding her apprehension.

"Come on, princess," I say. "I'll carry you if I have to."

"So cruel," she pouts, reluctantly rising to a seated position and gingerly sliding off the bed to pull on clothes.

"I know, but it's my job to take care of you, remember?"

CHAPTER 44

Addison

I WAKE to the sound of Asher's gentle breathing beside me and draw in a pained inhale.

I've been in denial about this day. I knew it was coming. It's been on my calendar for over a month now – the day I fly home to LA and Asher flies across the Atlantic.

It's bittersweet. I'm excited for him, and I know he's excited. As much as he tries to hide it, he's been working so damn hard. Sometimes I don't think the man sleeps.

I dread the ride to New York. I didn't change my flight and in hindsight, it would have been so much simpler to fly out of Boston. But now, I'll have to endure a long, four-hour countdown to our goodbye. Thirty minutes to the Boston airport would have been agonizing but efficient. We could have just ripped off the Band-Aid.

I've become so comfortable around him. Knowing he's sleeping by my side makes me feel safe and cared for. The nightmares have stopped and for once, I am able to breathe without the oppressive weight of my anxiety pressing down on my chest. I don't know how I'm going to fare next semester with him gone, especially if Anjali joins a sorority. I shouldn't have let myself become so reliant on him but I have.

My emotional, mental, and physical health have all improved with him consistently around.

He takes good fucking care of me. And now he's leaving.

I try to brush aside my worries because I don't want to unleash the fear and heartbreak I've bottled up over the past few months. Thanks to the constant distraction of my coursework and exams, there simply hasn't been time to think about the future and certainly no time to talk about it.

I crawl over him to go to the bathroom, and I wince at the notable soreness between my legs.

He absolutely destroyed me last night, just like I asked. He left me raw, and it hurt so good. But it wasn't the sex that ended me. It was what he said after.

"If you're asking me what I think about the idea of having a baby with you? I would say yes in a heartbeat."

I'm having a difficult time getting off the toilet because I keep replaying Asher's words in my mind – that, and I'm in a fair bit of discomfort this morning. He usually does a good job of toeing the line between pleasure and pain, but last night tipped the balance.

Maybe part of him was truly upset about Noah, and his jealously got the better of him?

No, something else was going on.

I carefully slink back to my dorm room only to find him awake and grinning at me with affection.

"How are you this morning?" he asks as I snuggle in next to him. I hum a response, not wanting to give an answer. There was no straightforward answer.

How am I? Terrified, nauseous, sick to my stomach. Dreading this car ride and this inevitable conversation about what will happen with us next semester when we're living on two different continents. Dreading the onslaught of tears I know will come when we say goodbye at the airport.

At least I know I'm not pregnant.

He trails a finger down my abdomen to the apex of my thighs.

"Mmm, no," I say a bit too quickly, pushing his hand away, and he laughs like he knows the reason behind my hesitation.

"A little tender down there this morning?"

"Very tender," I say sternly.

"Aww baby, I'm sorry," he says through gentle kisses. "But you wanted it so badly last night."

I squeeze my eyes shut. Obviously I remember, but hearing him say it back makes me cringe. I was feral. I was like a depraved animal finally released from its cage.

"You were so beautiful last night, baby girl," he says, sensing my embarrassment. "*We* were so beautiful together in that way. You are by far the best I've ever had in my life."

"And the best I ever will have," he adds.

"I want to ask you the number of women to which I'm compared but I also don't want to know," I blurt out before I can stop myself.

"You want to know my body count?" he laughs.

"No," I say with resolve, quickly changing my mind.

"I'll tell you if you really want to know!" He's smirking at me with a look that tells me he's a little too proud of his number.

"I don't want to know!"

His chuckle is deep and venomous as he nibbles at my ear with soft kisses.

"Well, for what it's worth, it's not as high as you might think."

I roll my eyes. I have no idea what "not that high" means to a twenty-two-year-old. I'm also keenly aware we're both clinging on to this irreverent conversation to delay the inescapable hard one we've managed to avoid until the last damn day.

"I guess we should get going," I say. I'm not sure if it's a question or a statement. I don't want to leave this tiny dorm room where we've spent so many nights together. Once we leave, our little fantasy bubble bursts and we'll be forced against our will to reckon with reality.

"Seems prudent," he says.

"Do you want to shower before we leave?" I ask.

"In that fucking bathroom?" he scoffs, tilting his head toward the communal men's bathroom down the hall. "Absolutely fucking not."

"It's not like the bathroom at your frat is any better!"

"Oh god no, it's worse! There is no getting clean in our frat bathrooms, not the ones on my floor anyway. Using those is just asking to get a staph infection."

"Wait, so where do you shower?" I ask.

"The gym, obviously. But sometimes I break into the senior wing of our frat and shower there. Those bathrooms are downright palatial in comparison. It's locked to keep the riff raff out, but Wyatt gave me the code."

"How does Wyatt know the code?"

"Because he's our incoming fraternity president. It's why he's not going abroad next semester – to fulfill his duties."

"Besides," Asher says, backtracking to my original question. "I smell like you and I'm not ready to wash your scent away. Not yet."

A hard lump rises in the back of my throat.

————

Asher goes back to his fraternity to collect his baggage while I shower. As touched as I am by Asher's desire to preserve my lingering smell on his skin, I felt like I desperately needed a shower for reasons beyond basic good hygiene practices.

I don't know what we're going to say on this car ride. But in the off chance it doesn't go the direction I expect, I can't board a transcontinental flight with the residue of Asher's cum still sticking to my legs.

What makes me the most nervous is the absence of those three small but pivotal words he has yet to say to me. We've only been sleeping together consistently for a few months, so I wouldn't have expected him to say them. But between telling me how desperately he needs me, saying it's his job to take care of me, and now the baby talk for fuck's sake, I guess I would have expected those three words to be thrown in the mix with the rest of it.

Maybe he doesn't think I'll say them back, but how I feel seems glaringly obvious.

The nausea churning in my stomach starts to reach a crescendo as we climb into his car. I'm quiet, staring out the window deep in thought. Truthfully, I'm too afraid to look at him or speak. I'm scared if I open my mouth, it'll be viewed as a signal I'm ready to talk about how we'll manage our relationship next semester. But I'm anything but ready.

People do long distance. People do it all the time, and it's fine. We'll make it work. It won't be so bad.

"When do you find out your final class standings?" he asks, breaking the silence.

"In the next day or so," I answer.

"Are you nervous?" he asks.

"Kind of," I respond.

"Is that why you're so quiet?"

I wipe the palms of my hands on my jeans.

"I'm quiet?" I ask.

"You haven't said a word since we started driving. You've just been curled up against the door looking out the window."

"It's not too late to change your flight, you know," Asher continues. "We can spend another night together."

"I really want to get home and see my mom," I answer.

"I know," he says quietly. "Can you at least scoot closer to me so I can hold your hand?"

I move closer to the center console, accepting his outstretched hand. He leans over, pulling our entwined hands up to his mouth and gives my hand a prolonged kiss.

"Are you getting excited now that it's finally time to leave for Oxford?" I ask, intentionally opening the door. *Might as well get it over with.*

"Very," he replies.

I watch his unflinching gaze.

"Feels like all I've been working toward is finally here," he goes on. "This semester kind of fucked me up though."

"Oh? How so? You were working around the clock."

"Only because I fell horribly behind, and the professor who's my mentor and the one who got me into Oxford threatened to pull the plug on his support."

"What?!" I say in shock. "That's bullshit. Why would he do that?"

"Because I told him in the spring I would hit certain milestones by the end of the summer and I didn't. And then I told him at the beginning of this semester I'd make up for lost time by October and I didn't do that either. So yeah, I fucked up pretty badly. Somehow, I pulled a rabbit out of my hat over the last few months, and he was satisfied I wouldn't embarrass him with this big-shot professor at Oxford. But he made it pretty clear I'm on thin ice and need to get my shit together."

"He sounds like a dick," I say.

"I mean," Asher sighs. "He was right. I was distracted and needed the ultimatum."

Distracted. I swallow at what I'm about to ask. Despite the tiny voice in my head screaming at me to shut up, I say it anyway.

"Why were you so distracted?"

Stupid. It was a stupid thing to ask.

"A few reasons," he humors me. "The whole dad dying thing threw me for a loop, and I'm not sure if you've noticed, but my friends and I party a lot."

I *have* very much noticed.

"And then you. You happened."

Oh god.

The nausea has gone from churning to a rapid boil, and my pulse quickens. I feel an overwhelming need to remove my hand from his, as if not having both hands tucked in my lap will throw me off balance.

"I… umm…," he pauses, and I'm convinced I'm going to throw up. "We need to have a conversation about us next semester."

"What about us?" I manage to squeak despite barely being able to breathe.

"You know, when I applied to Harvard, I knew I wanted to do this abroad program at Oxford. There's a professor there who runs a mentorship program for startup founders. He's super connected in the financial technology world, and all the startups he's mentored have gone on to participate in world-class accelerator programs, raised a shit ton of money, and many have gone on to become billion-dollar businesses. He's a big deal, very influential. He can make or break your success, so you can't risk working with him if you aren't focused."

Why is he telling me all this again? I already know this. I swallow.

"And the truth is, I've been very unfocused this past semester. I let other things get in my way and honestly, I feel as if I lost my purpose. I've been working on this startup since I was a teenager. It's been my dream to do something big with this opportunity, and Professor Friedman thinks I have an excellent shot at success. I mean, the potential of what I've built is huge – groundbreaking even. It could change the way the world monitors terrorism. But I can't get to where I want to go if I'm distracted."

He pauses his soliloquy, and I take the bait.

"So what are you saying?" I breathe.

"I guess what I'm saying is there can't be an *us* next semester. I won't be able to focus if I'm with you. Addison, I can't *not* think about you if we're together. I can't stop myself from thinking about you, what you're doing, how you're doing, who you're with. You know how jealous I get. I won't be able to focus. I'll spend all day thinking about calling you, wondering if you're thinking about me, and I just… I can't do it. I need to be selfish right now because I know I will forever regret what I could have become, what my startup could have become, if I don't."

"I need to do this, Addison, without us. I'm sorry."

I hear all the words he's saying but I'm no longer in my body. I left it halfway through his speech and have been floating above myself ever since. The devastating realization hits me like a wave crashing down on my head: Asher is *breaking up with me.*

Which is fucked, because I didn't realize we were officially together.

After everything he's put me through, *he's* breaking up with *me?*

And did he really, REALLY, just give me a bullshit "I love you but I love myself more" *speech?*

Then, another devastating realization crashes down like a fuck ton of bricks.

No, he didn't just give me that speech because he never said those words. He never told me he loved me, not once.

He never loved me.

The pain is so overwhelming, so consuming, I can't speak. I can't breathe. I can't even cry. My mind is racing but my voice is paralyzed.

After everything.

After last night and all the nights before. After everything that happened in LA over the summer. After Halloween and the morning after. After he begged me to give him a second chance. After he told me he wanted me to be the mother of his fucking children.

After that fucking PROMISE he made me.

It was a lie. All of it.

And to think I let myself believe I was his princess.

Not anymore, I'm not. Now, I'm just the distraction he has to get rid of.

Instinctively, I clutch at my chest. It feels like he picked up a jagged, rust-covered dagger and slammed it into my heart.

I can feel him looking over at me, glancing between my reaction and the road.

I am a goddamn fool. Ethan had tried to warn me, but I didn't listen. He had said Asher was the most selfish person he knew. I didn't want to believe him, but goddammit, Ethan was right.

Asher had *played me,* and I'm the fucking idiot who let him.

"Are you going to respond to what I just said?" he has the fucking nerve to ask.

I slowly turn to look at him, the monster sitting next to me who knowingly waited to have this conversation until the last possible fucking second, holding me hostage in his fucking car while he tells me I'm nothing more to him than a *distraction.*

"Am I going to *respond*?" I seethe. I can feel my hands shaking.

I look at the clock. Another thirty minutes until we get to JFK.

"Say something," he demands.

"Fuck you, Asher. FUCK. YOU."

I launch at him with the full depth of my fury.

"After everything you put me through this semester,

Asher… *this, THIS,* is what you do? I thought maybe, *maybe,* you were going to say let's take it slow, that we can try long distance but go into it knowing it might be too hard. *But this?"*

"You are unfuckingbelievable, Asher. You really are. Ethan was right about you. You LIED to me. You told me everything you knew I wanted to hear. But you're nothing more than a selfish prick of a fuckboy and I regret EVER letting you into my life."

The color has drained from his face.

"You don't mean that," he croaks.

I scoff in a bitter laugh.

"Don't tell me what I do and don't mean, Asher. I've heard enough of your bullshit for a lifetime."

"Addison, I'm…"

"STOP FUCKING TALKING TO ME," I scream. My breath is so shaky, I can barely see straight. I'm pleading with my body to hold it together long enough to make it out of this fucking obnoxious G-Wagen and into the airport, where I can have my nervous breakdown in peace.

We pull up to the curb, and I frantically unbuckle my seatbelt, prepared to jump out. He's already opened the trunk, and I race to grab my suitcase and get the hell away from him as fast as possible.

"Addison, STOP," he says, yanking me back before I can bolt inside.

"Don't *fucking touch me,*" I hiss through my teeth. "God forbid, Asher, I get in the way of your success. God forbid you think about anyone other than yourself."

"GO!" I scream at him, shoving so hard against his chest, he stumbles backward. "Go before I become a *distraction."*

The tears come now, fast and hot down my cheeks, clouding my vision as I fumble with the stupid handle of my suitcase.

"Do not call me, do not text me, do not so much as *dream about me*, Asher."

"You're a *liar*, Asher," I hiss at him through clinched teeth. "You made me believe you cared about me. You tricked me into thinking you *gave a shit*. But you never did. I trusted you, I had feelings for you, but *you*, all this time, just wanted to *fuck me*."

I practically spat those last two disgusting words at him and the look of shock and horror on his face almost has me fooled. But then I remember he's a liar, and it's time I deal this piece of shit his final blow.

"You were a *fucking mistake*."

I'm practically dragging my uncooperative suitcase behind me at this point, barreling through the clusters of people until I make it inside the airport.

There are many things I hate about airports but trying to find a bathroom suitable for a nervous breakdown in the departures area before you get through security has to be at the top of my list of complaints.

My phone buzzes, and of course he's calling me. I silence his call, only for the phone to ring again two seconds later.

"Fuck him," I say aloud before turning the whole thing off.

CHAPTER 45

Addison

THE OVERHEAD CABIN lights flicker on. I always forget how long the flight is from New York to Los Angeles and I'm exhausted.

I tried to sleep, but it was no use. The nausea I've felt since this morning hasn't subsided, and my mind oscillates between thoughts of running over Asher with my car and hating myself for getting involved with him in the first place.

How could I have been so stupid?

How could I have let myself become so emotionally attached to this man?

And to think I even gave this piece of shit a second chance.

The self-loathing almost trumps the heartbreak.

Almost.

My phone has been off for ten hours at this point. If it weren't for the need to tell my dad I've landed, I would conveniently, accidentally, leave it on the plane. I turn it on to see exactly what I expected.

Thirty-five missed voicemails from Asher.

Seventy-two texts.

One text from Anjali.

Addison, did you land yet? The results are up! We both fucking made it!! Welcome to the 5% club, bitch! Summer fellowship, here we come!

This news should make me ecstatic given how hard I worked. But the joy I should feel is woefully overshadowed by the loss I feel for Asher.

Tears threaten to appear again, and I shake them away.

No.

No, he does not get to take this from me.

I may have let him take all of me physically, but he does not get to take my fucking heart.

I'm taking it back.

CHAPTER 46

Asher

I KNEW the moment she turned her back on me and disappeared into the airport, I had fucked up.

I climb back into my car in a daze and start driving.

A mistake. She called me a mistake.

And she admitted she had feelings for me. I had been waiting so long to hear her say something, anything, to give me an indication of how she feels about me, about us.

It's too bad for me that she admitted to this truth in the same sentence where she accused me of being a lying asshole who just wanted to fuck her.

My fingers are going numb from my white-knuckled grip on the steering wheel. I hear my own breathing, choppy and wheezing. Car horns pierce the air, then fade away quickly, and suddenly I realize I'm driving over a hundred miles an hour, whizzing around traffic as if I'm on the streets of Monaco.

I take the next exit, unaware of my location but too distraught to give a shit. I pull into the first parking lot I see and stop.

Goddamn, it hurts so badly.

Why does this hurt so badly?

I claw at my chest, trying to rip away as much of my jacket and shirt as I can so my bleeding, broken fucking heart can breathe – as if oxygen is a salve for the excruciating pain I feel inside my ribcage.

An hour ago, we were breathing the same air. Six hours ago, we were lying next to each other in bed. Last night, I was inside her. For fuck's sake, I still *smell* like her.

And now she's fucking gone.

My mouth forms a sob, but no sound comes out. My throat is collapsing, my face is turning bright red, then blue, and I'm shaking so violently, I think I'm having a heart attack or seizure or both at the same time.

Then a noise rises up my esophagus – muffled at first, then louder and louder and louder until I scream.

I don't know how long I stay like that – seconds, minutes, hours. Screaming and screaming and screaming until I choke on my own tears.

I really said those despicable, ugly words to her, and I'll never be able to take them back. I called her a *distraction*. I'm deplorable.

And the hurt…

The hurt she wore across her face when she turned to walk away from me will haunt me forever. *I had made a promise to her.* She had trusted me to care of her and not be the selfish prick everyone says I am, *that her brother says I am.* But I had taken this beautiful, pure, innocent, trusting princess, and I broke her.

I deserve every name she called me.

I deserve to see her walk away.

I wouldn't blame her if she doesn't speak to me for the rest of my life.

On top of all the abominable things I said, what takes the fucking cake is I told her – the woman who I am positive is the love of my fucking life, the woman who I want to be the mother of my goddamn children – *that I didn't want her.*

I need to do this without us, I had said.

A fool. I'm a fucking fool.

I'm a fool who will spend the rest of my worthless life on my knees, begging for her back. I don't care how long it takes. I don't care if I lose myself trying.

TO BE CONTINUED

Addison and Asher's story continues in
Book 2 of the GOOD HURT series, where they are forced to reckon with the fallout of their separation while navigating the pull of unresolved inner demons and external temptations. But unfortunately for our two heartbroken lovers, a new danger has come to town, and he's not letting go...

About the Author

Summer Robert is a recovering corporate girlie turned weaver of angsty, dark romance stories that are as salacious as they are suspenseful. After leaving the corporate world behind, Summer published her debut dark romance series, GOOD HURT, and hopes she can continue to delight the dark romance community with her extra spicy and entertaining novels (plus unhinged posts for her BookTok friends). Most importantly, she's a mom of two small humans and one small, vicious, and spiteful yorkipoo. Summer currently resides in Los Angeles, and although she is originally a native Ohioan from a small farm town, she will forever call Los Angeles her home.

Follow me on social media and join my newsletter for updates about my next book! To see all I have published (and for extra goodies), visit my website, SummerRobert-Books.com.

instagram.com/summerrobertwrites
tiktok.com/@summerrobertwrites